SPECIAL MESSAGE TO READERS

This book is published under the auspices of

THE ULVERSCROFT FOUNDATION

(registered charity No. 264873 UK)

Established in 1972 to provide funds for research, diagnosis and treatment of eye diseases. Examples of contributions made are: —

A Children's Assessment Unit at Moorfield's Hospital, London.

•

Twin operating theatres at the Western Ophthalmic Hospital, London.

•

A Chair of Ophthalmology at the Royal Australian College of Ophthalmologists.

•

The Ulverscroft Children's Eye Unit at the Great Ormond Street Hospital For Sick Children, London.

You can help further the work of the Foundation by making a donation or leaving a legacy. Every contribution, no matter how small, is received with gratitude. Please write for details to:

THE ULVERSCROFT FOUNDATION,
The Green, Bradgate Road, Anstey,
Leicester LE7 7FU, England.
Telephone: (0116) 236 4325

In Australia write to:

THE ULVERSCROFT FOUNDATION,
c/o The Royal Australian and New Zealand
College of Ophthalmologists,
94-98 Chalmers Street, Surry Hills,
N.S.W. 2010, Australia

BETRAYAL OF INNOCENCE

Annie works hard to keep her father from the poorhouse. However, she is wracked with guilt as she watches her friend, Georgette Davey, being used by Lady Constance. Annie longs to escape her life at the Hall, taking Georgette with her — but how? The arrival of the mysterious doctor, Samuel Speer, adds to her dilemma as Annie's concern for her friend grows. Georgette's innocence has been betrayed, but Annie is unaware of the threat that hangs over her own.

Books by Valerie Holmes
in the Linford Romance Library:

THE MASTER OF MONKTON MANOR
THE KINDLY LIGHT
HANNAH OF HARPHAM HALL
PHOEBE'S CHALLENGE

VALERIE HOLMES

BETRAYAL OF INNOCENCE

Complete and Unabridged

LINFORD
Leicester

First published in Great Britain in 2005

First Linford Edition
published 2006

British Library CIP Data

Holmes, Valerie
Betrayal of innocence.—Large print ed.—
Linford romance library
1. Love stories
2. Large type books
I. Title
823.9′2 [F]

ISBN 1–84617–450–3

Published by
F. A. Thorpe (Publishing)
Anstey, Leicestershire

Set by Words & Graphics Ltd.
Anstey, Leicestershire
Printed and bound in Great Britain by
T. J. International Ltd., Padstow, Cornwall

This book is printed on acid-free paper

1

'Father, I will try to call again tomorrow,' Annie said then kissed her father's brow, before she tucked his blanket around his legs.

'I'm no use to anyone. You should put me in the poorhouse and be done with it, girl.'

His words hurt Annie but she knew they were genuine and not merely spoken to gain sympathy.

'I'll never do that to you, Father. You'll become strong again. Dr Brown has told us so.' She kissed him once more. 'We'll be together soon, you'll see.'

'We can always pray it is so. You put me to shame. You have so much faith and I so little.'

His large frame slumped in the chair.

'Father, you are ill, so it is not lack of faith that holds you back, but your poor health.'

Annie wrapped her shawl around herself.

'Be gone, daughter, and I'll be fine. Don't listen to the mumblings of an old fool.'

'Until tomorrow,' Annie answered.

She watched him force a smile on to his face and nod at her.

'Mornin', dearie.'

The smile soon faded from Annie's face when she heard the high, trill voice of Muriel Hankin. She noticed the look of relief on her father's face as the woman bustled into the cottage.

'How are we today?'

Muriel smiled fleetingly at Annie as she passed her in the doorway. She walked straight over to Annie's father.

'Feeling any better, Thomas?' she asked.

Her father shrugged dismissively, his eyes focussing on the pot that she placed on the hearth.

'This'll warm you up. Our Arthur brought us a big hare. I saved some for you, Thomas. A man needs a good meal to sustain his strength.'

She turned and looked at Annie who was still standing on the threshold.

'Go on, lass. You don't be worrying about your pa. You get on. We'll be fine.'

Annie nodded and reluctantly set out from the old cottage, where her father had lived all his working life, and headed for the servants' quarters at Hallam Hall. Her heart felt heavy with worry for him, but underneath, another emotion was rising within her. She felt ashamed of it because she had much to thank Muriel for, yet jealousy and resentment mixed, gnawing at her because the hearth was her mother's place and not Muriel's.

Annie missed her mother still. One year had already passed since her death and shortly after, her father's health deteriorated so quickly that he couldn't work the land any longer. Week in, week out, he seemed to lose his strength, despite his medicine. He was beyond his middle years and Annie admitted to herself reluctantly he was now ageing fast, but it was so hard for her to take on their well-being because he had always been so strong.

It was all she could do to keep up with the payment to Dr Brown for his medicine, and pay the rent on the cottage to the estate for Lord Hallam. Thank goodness that Cook at the hall was a kindly soul and a good friend to them. She helped a lot by giving Annie vegetables needed to make the basic broth on which they relied.

If she could just work long enough at the hall to pay off the arrears on the rent that her father owed since he had stopped farming, then she could do what her heart was set on — teach the village children to read and write like her father had taught her.

As Annie approached the hall, day was just dawning. She thought she saw someone, or a movement by the chapel doorway. The small church of St Aidan nestled in its own garden to the right of the castellated hall. She stopped and stared, but saw nothing other than a squirrel run up an old oak tree. Annie crossed over the cobbled stones that led to the kitchen entrance at the back of the hall.

'Thank goodness, you're here at last!'

Cook ran over to greet Annie as she entered.

'Why, what's wrong?' Annie asked as she removed her shawl and folded it neatly.

'Lady Constance wants to see you as soon as you arrive back from the dairy.'

Cook nodded to her as a young maid left the kitchen with a tray set for Lord Hallam.

'The dairy? Oh, right. Churning butter?' Annie asked, wondering how involved Cook's lie had been, covering for her, as she was supposed to stay in the servants' quarters, especially now.

'If you like, dear. We didn't get that far. She don't care what you're doin' as long as you're there when she calls. You weren't, by the way.'

Cook beamed at her friend.

'Best be goin' up before she sends the

dragoons out searchin' for you.'

Cook stopped smiling and Annie wasted no time in running up the servants' stairs to the back corridor on the first floor of the hall.

Georgette Davey entered the large, oak-panelled corridor as Annie appeared at the top of the narrow stairs. Annie took a sharp intake of breath as she looked unbelievingly at the state of her friend and former governess at the hall. Georgette, the poor woman, was pale, drawn and had no business being where she could be seen. Annie rushed towards her and couldn't help being overwhelmed by a feeling of sadness at the current state the young woman was in.

Downstairs, Lady Constance left the library, crossed the large hallway and started to ascend the main staircase to the oak landing. Annie heard the movement of the fine silk skirts as her ladyship approached. Each step that made the noise of her movement was becoming clearer, meaning only one thing — that trouble was descending and poor Georgette was in no condition to hurry back to her room before being seen.

Annie ran over to Georgette, who was leaning unsteadily against the oak-panelled hallway, her hand automatically resting on the unborn child who kicked energetically within her. Annie knew she should not be there but, as the birth approached, the solitary life Georgette had had, coupled with her increasing fear as her time neared, must have made her put all reasoning aside.

'You know you're not allowed to come out of your room, Georgette!'

Annie spoke quietly, but firmly, not just out of concern for her friend's condition, but for the impact it could have on her own precarious position. Sorry she may be for the poor woman who had played so easily into the perilous hand of Lady Constance, but she, too, had more to consider than herself. She had to keep her father out of the poorhouse, debtors' prison or even the madhouse if that was what those in charge wished.

Should Lady Constance discover Georgette had wandered into the corridor that led straight to the upper central landing, they would both be in for a sharp rebuke. Constance, Annie was well aware, was not a lady who took kindly to her orders being disobeyed. Georgette was intended to be spending her confinement in secret, locked away in an unused room at the back of Hallam Hall.

'I was restless, Annie. The pains, they're growing stronger and I was all alone.'

With each spasm, Georgette stopped to catch her shortening of breath.

'I feel frightened. It's like an oppressive darkness, a gloom that comes over me. Annie, I can't help it. I'm really scared. I just feel like something's going awfully wrong. I don't know what, but it is, I can sense it!'

'Hush, Georgette Davey. If anyone

were to hear you they'd be thinking that you're a witch. I can't do with people thinking they sense things. You're just imagining it. It's part of your condition, that and too much time on your hands.'

Annie realised she was being patronising but she had to talk her down, keep the woman calm for both their sakes. Then Annie smiled sweetly at her, remembering the poor, unborn baby within her friend.

'Besides, you've had too much learnin' for a woman, givin' you ideas.'

Georgette managed a small laugh at Annie, because that was a long-standing joke between them. Both women had had an education and both had been told at different times how it was wasted on a woman's brain.

'Honestly, Georgette, all women fear the first time that they give birth. It's natural.'

Annie tried to smile and give some confidence to Georgette, but what she was really thinking was that Georgette's instincts were more astute than the young woman had realised. She had more to worry about than presenting the world with another bastard. Annie prayed her friend carried a boy child. Every night, she prayed it would be, for it was the only way she could be saved, and at least the baby would have a good life.

'What do you think you are doing here, girl?'

The sharpness of Lady Constance's voice shook Annie, and so did Georgette's reaction as she physically jumped back a step. Annie put a protective arm around her to steady her.

'I'm sorry, Lady Constance, I . . . '

Georgette tried to explain to her beautiful, young mistress why she had ventured outside the room, hoping, it seemed, that she would appeal to her better nature. Annie could have told her friend she was wasting her breath, as Lady Constance didn't have one. Instead, Georgette doubled up with a sudden pain, so intense that each wave that followed threatened to bring the troubled young woman to her knees.

'Must I keep you under lock and key?' Constance snapped at her, glaring at Annie who had begged her mistress not to lock her in when she had first put Georgette into secret confinement.

Annie was glad it would be over soon. She could not keep up the deception much longer.

'God,' she prayed to herself, 'just let it be a boy!'

The anger in Lady Constance's words had obviously made Georgette feel ashamed. Annie looked on in despair as her friend's face flushed red.

'You are an ungrateful wretch!' Lady Constance continued.

Annie looked upon her as a bully, using the power and position she held maliciously. She could see that she had the upper hand and was intimidating her vulnerable prey. She still continued to harangue Georgette.

'Did you not realise the stupidity of your actions? Have I not been kindness itself to you? If your presence here was discovered, I would have no choice but to turn you out for a harlot, for that is what you would be labelled by every decent member of society — the governess who had fallen so low that she carried the lord's illegitimate child!'

Lady Constance sniffed as if disgusted at the thought. Georgette gasped at the harshness of her lady's words.

'But . . . ' Georgette turned to face her lady, with a hint of defiance showing in her eyes.

'Don't think for a moment that you could get away with serving a bastardy order on my dear lord and husband.'

Lady Constance's eyes stared directly and accusingly at Georgette's.

'I wouldn't do that, but you know that the child is his,' Georgette replied.

Annie wanted to intervene and rescue her friend from Constance's venom, but she dared not. Annie hated the feeling of being a coward in any way but she, too, was in a precarious position.

'For propriety's sake, he could never admit it! Do you think they would believe that in a moment of grief and weakness he had succumbed to your charms? Think, woman! You're a fallen wench, and Lord Robert is a gentleman.' Lady Constance stared hard at Georgette, who shrank from her gaze. 'You would be declared mad before you even made the charge a formality.'

'But it wasn't like that. I mean . . .'

'I have no wishes to know how it was! Spare my feelings on this matter, please. Have you no respect at all?'

She turned her head away as if the vulgarity of the topic was too much for her, then turned around again to face Georgette accusingly.

'Or do you think only of yourself and your own desires?'

Lady Constance emphasised the last word.

Annie braced herself. She silenced her tongue before it placed her in as much danger as poor, naïve Georgette. Annie thought her mistress was the biggest, most talented hypocrite she had ever met, and she had met quite a few. For all her indignation, though, Annie also knew Lady Constance could have her father thrown into the debtors' gaol in minutes, should she wish to, so she worked for her loyally even though she felt she had sold her very soul into bondage with the devil.

Annie often thought that Constance should have lived in France, then her ladyship would have got what all her class deserved! Annie subdued a smile as she listened to her lady's hypocritical words and wondered how she'd have lied her way out of a visit to Madame Guillotine! No doubt, Annie thought, she would have succeeded somehow. Annie shrugged off any guilt she may have felt at the severity of her wishes when Constance continued to berate the unfortunate Georgette.

'How else could you prove the child was his?' Lady Constance continued to chastise Georgette, who was nearly in tears.

'No, Miss Davey, you have been blessed with my kindness and charity.

Now, return to your room and do not venture beyond it again!'

Lady Constance pointed to the door at the end of the corridor.

'Return without further ado!'

'But the lonely months have seemed endless, almost like being in gaol,' Georgette tried to explain her actions, to gain her mistress's understanding.

None was forthcoming. Lady Constance merely pointed again towards the door of her room. Georgette lowered her eyes slightly.

'I'm sorry, milady. I was not thinking.'

She had no more fight left within her.

'Well, now we have established that fact, do as I say!'

Lady Constance's dark eyes peered into the moist pools that were Georgette's until the woman turned away dejectedly. Slowly, she managed to straighten up and return to her room. Annie walked with her, determined that one day soon, she would find some way to unseat the horrible, nasty Lady Constance. Rich or not, she was harder than any wench Annie had ever met.

Georgette made her way slowly down the corridor. Annie cupped her elbow, letting go only to open the door. Georgette took one step towards her bed, tripped on the clipped rag mat and fell to her knees with a deafening scream of pain. Annie heard the door slam shut behind them.

Lady Constance had left when Georgette was still on her knees on the old clip mat. Annie had left to fetch and carry water to the room then she heard the key turn behind her once she had returned.

'Bitch!' Annie muttered to herself but Georgette was making too much noise for the word to be heard.

They were both locked inside the room, no doubt until the birth was over, she thought. Annie prayed harder than ever as she busied herself with the near hysterical woman. She'd helped a horse to foal once, but she had no birthing experience with humans.

The pain of the following hours melted into one long nightmare. Annie and Georgette were trapped in a battle of survival, that only the cry of a new-born baby would finally end. What seemed like an age later, a baby's head finally emerged.

'Push, Georgie, push!'

Annie issued instructions as though she had delivered many a child, instinct replacing fear. Finally, the babe slipped out on to the towel.

'Damnation, it's a girl!' Annie exclaimed.

Her worst fear had been realised. What would save Georgette now? She had no idea. God was her only hope, if he had heard any of Annie's prayers.

'What did you say?'

Georgette's faint voice made Annie feel angry at her lack of sensitivity. Poor Georgette, she thought. She was an innocent pawn in all of this, so beautiful, so intelligent, yet so stupidly naïve. A girl of her breeding deserved better, Annie thought, even if she had been the youngest of five daughters.

'Look, Georgette, you have a beautiful girl.'

Annie, the only servant trusted with the knowledge of Georgette's confinement, held the child up to face her mother as she raised herself on the small bed to see the beautiful baby.

'I'll call her Bethany, Annie.'

She smiled, visibly exhausted and in need of a deep sleep.

As the baby cried, the door was unlocked and opened. Lady Constance stood silently in the doorway.

'Is it over?' she asked without coming into the room.

Annie saw her wince as she stood looking around. Lady Constance covered her mouth with a lace handkerchief after glancing at the soiled, blood-stained clothes that lay in a discarded heap on the floor.

'Yes, milady. Georgette and the baby are both well,' Annie answered, not wanting to answer the next question that she knew would come.

'What is it, Fletcher?' Lady Constance demanded.

Annie hesitated and muffled her

words so her reply was inaudible.

'I have a beautiful daughter, milady,' Georgette announced excitedly, raising the child in her arms. 'Look, Lady Const . . . '

The door banged shut, leaving Georgette stunned, staring beseechingly at the face of her only friend.

'What does this mean, Annie? Why did she go away like that?'

Georgette held the baby to her breast protectively, and Annie could see the feeling of foreboding return to her friend's eyes.

'You must rest, Georgette. You'll need all your strength.'

Annie gathered up the soiled clothes into a large bundle and moved towards the door. She had to get out and think.

'Tell me, Annie, what is happening? You're my friend. Help me. Help us.'

Georgette was staring intensely at the slim figure in front of her. Annie put the bundle of cloths down, wiped her hands on her apron, and sat on the edge of the bed, stroking the child's cheek. Her eyes were moist and she sniffed.

'Listen to what I have to tell you.'

She glanced towards the door then lowered her voice to a whisper.

'They wanted a boy, Georgette, an heir. Lady Constance can't have children, not anymore, and since young Robert died, his lordship is desperate for another son. So she let him have a child by a healthy, intelligent young woman — you, Georgette.'

Annie was looking straight at her, but could see Georgette was unable to grasp the enormity of what she was being told. That meant she had been a stupid, gullible fool, duped by his lordship, used.

'No, it can't be so. He was drunk. It was an accident, a moment of madness. We both had too much wine, after young Robert's accident. It was my tragedy. He doted on the boy. Everyone was so emotional, and I lost my position with the child when he died. Poor Robert, he was so weak, and I had such affection for him. I should never have left myself in such a vulnerable position that my pity for his lordship could have led to . . . to . . . '

Georgette looked at the tiny face nestling contentedly against her skin.

'He had no memory of it, but Lady Constance found out. She helped me. She said she would find me a position in the country, somewhere I could say I was a widow, or some such.'

Georgette looked at her baby and swallowed hard.

'Oh, dear God, Annie, what am I to do? We have nothing.'

2

Annie washed, took a tray up to her friend, who slept, and saw the child was wrapped safely in clean clothes. Then she headed for the open air. She had been trapped in that room for so many hours and her head ached with the stress of it all, and at the distress of her friend's situation.

She walked across the grounds to the track that would lead to the village. Her father would be in his cottage. At least her job ensured he had a roof over his head and broth above the fire in the inglenook. She paused momentarily as she saw a strange horse tethered outside. She felt anger rising up within her. Who was bothering him now? She burst into the room, striding over the threshold, to be confronted by a man, well attired, smartly dressed and bent double over her father who lay on his cot.

'Unhand him! Who are you and what business do you have here?'

The startled visitor looked round, but did not remove his hand from her father's wrist. He stood straight.

'Excuse me, please, for not formally introducing myself. I am a doctor, and you are?'

His manner was calm, completely unperturbed by her presence, confident even. Annie closed the door behind her.

'I know he is sick. I am his daughter!' she replied but gave no name.

'Then why have I not been summoned before now?'

His manner was still calm. He stared enquiringly at her with his deep brown eyes and raised eyebrow. Annie found it annoying.

'Because . . . ' Annie hesitated momentarily. 'We have only enough money to pay Dr Brown for his regular medicine!'

The doctor rolled the blanket back over her father.

'Let me introduce myself properly. I

am Samuel Speer, miss, doctor of the village, and am new to the parish. May I see what Dr Brown has been giving your father?'

The man looked at her as if he expected his request to be obeyed without question.

'Dr Brown is our doctor. The village is not large enough to warrant having two,' she answered without moving to fetch anything.

'Annie, he is trying to help me. Muriel asked him to call . . . ' Her father's voice was weak.

Muriel, Annie was going to say, had no business interfering, but she realised that the woman only meant well. Annie just wished she wouldn't constantly interfere in things that did not concern her — like her father.

Reluctantly, Annie fetched the bottle of elixir and held it out to the stranger. She wanted to ask him to leave, yet there was something about his attitude that seemed to command respect. He took the bottle, removing the cork, and sniffed it suspiciously then shook his head with what seemed annoyance.

'I strongly suggest you do not continue with this. I cannot call it medicine.'

'Why? We paid good money for it!'

Annie was outraged. She had worked, almost slaved, for Lady Constance for a year in order to pay the rent on the small cottage and then for this medicine. Now this stranger was telling her it was not needed.

'Dr Brown says it will give him his strength back. It . . . '

'Dr Brown is under investigation. He is no longer practising in this village. I'm sorry, I have no wish to cause you distress. However, I suspect he has been profiting from your ignorance and . . . '

Annie put both hands on her hips, standing square to the handsome, educated man in front of her and defiantly interrupted him.

'How dare you!'

Annie was furious but her head ached so much that she almost felt faint. All the tension and fear that had built up in her during the birth of Georgette's baby threatened to overwhelm her.

'I am not ignorant!'

'. . . and vulnerability, I was going to say, not to insult you. You are not educated with knowledge of medicine, miss. That is all I inferred. Are you all right, miss?'

He rushed forward as Annie reached out for the back of a chair to break her fall. She landed, not on the stone-flagged floor, but against the doctor's chest as he wrapped both his arms around her and took her weight.

The room seemed to spin around and she felt herself being lifted bodily up into the air. It was with some embarrassment that she felt her back against her familiar bed. Her head ached. She kept her eyes closed as the world around her seemed to move. She breathed in sharply as the stranger's hands loosened her dress.

'Stop it!'

Her voice was no more than a

whisper. She opened her eyes as a foul-smelling substance was wafted under her nostrils.

'You are perfectly decent, and you can trust me. I am a doctor, and I can also assure you, a man of ethics, unlike Dr Brown, whose morals, shall we say, are questionable.'

His words were spoken softly. Annie opened her eyes, with great effort.

'What is wrong with my father if the elixir is no good?'

'I think he has had a malady that has been prolonged by the concoction within the bottle. I suspect that with a good diet he would regain his previous health. He has in effect been drugged.'

There was a softness in his eyes as he looked at her, almost as if he regretted having to tell her the truth. Annie felt tears roll down her cheeks. He stroked her brow and smoothed her hair softly, like a child being comforted.

'I've been paying a man to poison him?' Annie repeated as anger fuelled her wits.

'No, not poison, subdue. I suppose if he had had a greater dose and over a longer time, the effects could have been worse. You were not to know, though, so please don't be too harsh on yourself.'

He smiled at her kindly and Annie felt herself blush slightly. She looked up at the handsome face that stared down at her from the side of her bed.

'Can you reverse the effect?'

'I think within a week or so he will have recovered from the effects of it in his system. However, my concern is now for you. You should rest. You look exhausted.'

'Rest! I can't possibly. I must return to the hall. I have much to do. Someone has to pay the rent. I . . . '

Annie sat bolt upright, swung her legs on to the floor to stand up, forgetting about her state of attire. The dress dropped to her waist, revealing her loosely-fitting shift.

'Oh . . . I . . . '

Annie bent down quickly, grabbing at her dress, fumbling to cover herself up, but she had moved too quickly again and only served to swoon once more. Dr Speer held her up. She felt the strength of his hands on her sides, almost touching her naked skin through her thin shift. He stepped behind her, helping her to fasten up her dress once more.

'I'm a doctor, miss. I am familiar with the female form in all its various shapes and conditions.'

'Perhaps so, sir, but I am unaccustomed to undressing in front of strangers,' Annie snapped back as she pulled herself straight.

'I am indeed happy to hear it, miss. It would be such a waste of a young maid was it any other way.'

Annie turned around carefully and faced him. She was sure she caught a glimmer of a smile on his face, but chose not to look at him further. Instead, she went to her father's bedside. He was sleeping soundly. She checked that he had enough broth to eat, and left some of Cook's bread on the table for him.

'I can't stay. I have to return to the hall. I'm needed there,' Annie explained.

'Are you not needed here, miss?' he asked as he picked up his bag.

'Yes, but until Father can work again, I need to earn the money to pay the cottage's rent to the estate. Hopefully soon, it will be different . . . ' She thought about Georgette. 'For everyone,' she added.

'I could visit the hall and explain your situation to Lady Constance Hallam. I'm sure she would look kindly on you.'

'No! Please don't. I know you mean well but honestly it would be best not to disturb her ladyship with my problems. Thank you all the same.'

Annie gestured towards the doorway.

'If you insist,' he said.

Annie did not think he was surprised by her refusal.

'I will check on him in the morning,' he said as he opened the cottage door.

'How much do we owe you, sir?'

She forced herself to look him in the eye, even though her feeling of embarrassment had not left her.

'Not a thing.' He smiled warmly at her.

'We don't need charity,' Annie began, but the stranger raised his hand to stop her.

'Yes, miss, sadly you do. A man of my profession has wronged you. Allow me to correct a wrong, make right that wrong, this once.'

Annie was speechless, but nodded her humble acceptance of his kindness.

'Good day, miss. I shall call again.'

He placed his hat on his head and mounted his horse. Annie waved goodbye to him. Deep inside her she wanted him to stay. She hoped that the man who had seen more of her than any other in her life would return soon.

3

Lady Constance sat with her head bowed before the altar in the small, private chapel by the side of the hall. She picked at the skirt of her expensive silk gown, still deeply annoyed at the birth of the girl and the disobedience of the two women. Still, she would not have to put up with them for long.

Constance heard nothing. Frustrated by her own display of piety, and angered by the foolish woman upstairs, she stifled a yawn. The gloved hand that touched her neck made her close her eyes as she leaned her head towards its gentle touch.

'You came. I was beginning to doubt your commitment to us.'

Her voice was cold, betraying little emotion.

'Never, ever doubt that, my dear, sweet Constance. I would travel to the end of the known world just to spend an evening in your delightful company.'

'Not beyond, Edgar?' Her voice lifted slightly, disclosing an element of humour.

'For a night in your sensuous company I would travel into monster-filled, uncharted waters, do not doubt.'

He kissed her neck eagerly. Then he pulled back.

'Do you have what I need?'

The cloaked figure sat down in the pew behind her. Constance could feel his breath, teasing her. Her body longed to have him make love to her just one last time. She knew she had precisely what he needed, but that was a fancy her head would not allow her body to satisfy. He was dangerous, which was part of his attraction, but she had too much to lose. The choice was simple. Either she forfeit her lifestyle or his life. Simply no choice at all, she decided — he had to die.

'Of course, my love, have I ever let you down?'

'Not yet, and I?'

His answer showed their mutual distrust of each other but in the business they shared together, they needed absolute trust, yet, being human, that was an impossible state to achieve. Lady Constance's eyes focussed upon the faces of the saints as they stared accusingly down upon her from above the altar. She smiled defiantly back at them, conscience untouched, heart of stone.

'Never.'

'Close your eyes, my lady,' he whispered, his voice low and inviting.

She let her lids meet and felt the warmth of his lips against hers. He was, had been, a passionate lover. Shame, she thought, because she would miss him, but he had become a risk, a huge liability. Besides, there would be others. Constance was young and she had her future to consider.

'Here.'

He placed a small letter in her hand and she produced a purse that he quickly put in an inside pocket.

'When will you return, my dear Edgar?'

Lady Constance breathed heavily as she spoke, her voice deliberately filled with desire. The passion in it was genuine, and it was in her interest to let it show. He must not suspect a thing.

'No names. I shall be back sooner than you can imagine, my pretty one. You will be mine soon, before you ever dreamed possible. Your stout old lord will be nothing but a memory, a nightmare, and I will be the essence of your dreams personified. On that I give you my word.'

'As a gentleman?'

Lady Constance smiled broadly to herself. She knew who Edgar was — a lord's son, and an adventurer, but to her he was a lovesick fool!

'Of course, until then . . . '

Silence followed. Lady Constance turned around and, as she expected, he had gone. How dramatic, she thought sardonically.

'I will belong to no man!' she muttered under her breath.

If only he were going to live that long, she muttered under her breath. If only he were going to live that long, she may have let him humour her one final time. Her lord took what he wanted of her in the bedchamber and she from his purse, but Edgar had been the most considerate of lovers. Constance had been keen to learn. She smiled at the thought and dipped a curtsey at the altar before turning her back to it, laughing as she walked away briskly.

* * *

'Nine months! Nine months, Constance, and for what? A girl!'

Lady Constance had dismissed the servants as she watched her husband stride up and down the breakfast room. He knocked a silver candlestick off the table with his fist.

'Damnation! Shall I never have another heir? This is too bad, Constance. I pay for her board and give her our best food and she produces a girl! She did have the best, didn't she?'

He looked sternly at his wife. Her eyes never gave any hint of a lie as she answered.

'Why, of course, my dear.'

Constance had watched the candlestick fall to the floor. She was used to his temper.

'My sweet, dear, Edmund.'

She walked over to him and kissed his forehead tenderly, for she was taller than he. Where his stature was portly, she was elegant and tall, with a sharp wit and wisdom beyond her twenty-two years.

'She is of no use to you, my lord. You can do better. We'll seek out a more suitable wench. Then you can have your heir. This time I may have to be more selective than using what is convenient. It may be more expensive but we can buy silence and then there will be no loose ends to tie up.'

He almost purred with contentment at the touch of her hands. He was ruthless and powerful in business, yet Constance could make him whimper like a child or buy her anything she willed, but she could not bear him a child, or at least that is what she would have him believe.

'She let you down, Edgar, an ungrateful wench. She is not worthy of you and neither is her child. How can you be sure the child is yours anyway? If she gave herself to you, my love, she could equally have given herself to another after you.'

He nodded in agreement.

'What do we do with her now? I don't want a fallen woman living openly under my roof. We'd have every beggar in Yorkshire wanting my charity. I cannot abide the thought of a scandal to befall my great name. No, I will not have it. Besides, we do not need any attention of that sort drawn to us. We have too much to lose, Constance.'

He stared intensely at her.

'We are going to be great. Soon you can forget the cold North, my darling. You will adorn my arm at Court, whilst it still exists. Ours is the future for the taking. This may have been a mistake, but it must end cleanly, and now.'

'She will be gone this night. From tomorrow you shall never see her face again. No, go into York, dear Edmund, and meet your friends then return to me refreshed.'

Lady Constance smiled broadly at him, knowing that when the coach returned he would be so drunk he would sleep for at least two days, only waking to gorge or drink some more. It would give her ample time to think over the minor problem of his heir.

He pressed his lips against hers and swept her into his arms. He was besotted with her. Constance knew he was no fool, but a strong and powerful man. It had been easy to remove her predecessor, Lady Agnes, but now she had to protect her own position. She smiled at him endearingly until his face disappeared into her bosom. Then her customary hardness returned.

A knock on the door separated them. Lady Constance quickly took up a casual pose by the window, whilst Lord Edmund berated the poor servant who had unwittingly disturbed his pleasure.

'What is it?' he bellowed.

'My lord, your coach is ready,' Jeremiah, a young servant, announced nervously.

'Did I order it? Hmm? Answer me, boy! Were you born stupid?' He sighed heavily. 'I forget, of course you were, but I expect better.'

'My lord, I sent for your carriage for you, so that you may attend to business at your club.' Lady Constance smiled at him as she accompanied him to the driveway.

'My dear, you are heaven sent to me. I shall be back tomorrow. I leave all in your capable hands.

He kissed his wife's hand and took his leave. She watched her husband's back disappearing into a coach that would take him far away from her. She strode boldly back into the house and as she passed the servant, she glanced sideways.

'Come, Jeremiah, I have work for you to do.'

4

Two hours later, Georgette jumped anxiously as Lady Constance entered her room, followed by a young boy carrying a tray.

'Dear Georgette, do not look so alarmed. My dear child, what must you be thinking of me?'

Lady Constance sat on the only chair in the corner of the room. She smiled sweetly at the baby but made no move to touch it. Instead she carefully arranged the skirt of her dress.

Georgette held her baby firmly to her bosom. She looked pale against the severe black governess's dress she had squeezed herself back into, yet was standing nervously by the small window.

'My dear child, sit down before you fall.'

Constance pointed to the bed, raised her hand and signalled for the servant,

Jeremiah, to bring in the tray. He placed it on the small table next to the chair and was quickly dismissed. Georgette stared at the woman she had looked upon as her salvation, her only means of survival for her and her baby, and plainly now doubted every good thought she had ever had about her.

'I had hoped, Georgette, that it would not come to this. If you had delivered my lord a boy then perhaps I could have persuaded him to provide for you both, but as it is, you had a girl. So we are left to our own devices as to what to do next.'

She sighed and cupped her hands together on her lap.

'You planned to steal my child!' Georgette uttered the words incredulously.

Lady Constance sighed heavily.

'Georgette Davey, drink your warm milk before it goes cold.'

She gestured to a porcelain beaker on the tray. Georgette looked at it longingly, but did not move a hand towards it.

'You have been the most fortunate girl in all of Yorkshire. You seduce my husband, carry an illegitimate child, are provided for under my very roof and you accuse me of being dishonourable, a thief even!'

Lady Constance's voice rose dramatically as she uttered the last two words.

'My girl, your child could have been the next lord of Hallam Hall, and in time much, much more, if only you had provided his lordship with a boy.'

Georgette cringed involuntarily.

'I believed in you.'

'You are an ungrateful wretch! Now, drink this milk before I have it taken away and both you and the child thrown out of my home into the gutter where I am starting to believe you belong!'

Georgette took the milk and sipped the sweet, warm liquid with relish, still holding tightly to her sleeping baby.

'Good, you relax now and listen to me. This is what we are going to do . . . '

Lady Constance's voice drifted away as the room blurred before Georgette's eyes. She fell on to the bed with her baby still in her arms, spilling the drugged milk all over the newly-changed linen. Constance watched the motionless body of Georgette and the screaming child and smiled.

'Jeremiah.' She called the boy back. 'Take them with Amos to the moor beyond the abbey ruins, well beyond the moor road. Do it tonight. Tell Amos to use his natural discretion.'

'Do what, ma'am?'

The youth's eyes were open wide, fixed on the tiny human who lay screaming in distress on the bed. The strike, which landed across Jeremiah's cheek, cracked like a whip, yet he did not flinch.

'I am a lady, not the cook!'

Constance's dark eyes peered into his. Knowing his place, he looked at his feet, ignoring the whimpers of the discarded baby as it lay on the bed.

'Never call me ma'am. You address

me as my lady at all times. You take them there, make sure you are not seen, and leave no track that will lead back here when you return with Amos.'

Jeremiah froze, but looked as if he would wish to speak.

'What is it now, boy?'

'Tonight is the ghost night!'

'What nonsense is this?' Constance's face turned suddenly into a broad smile and laughter. 'All souls. Jeremiah, I have told you before about listening to Cook's tales. Now, follow my orders, or you shall join them. Do you understand me?'

Jeremiah nodded nervously and, as soon as his lady left, he picked up the child, singing quietly, watching as she fell silent with the soothing momentum as he rocked the baby gently in his arms.

⋆ ⋆ ⋆

'Amos's gone for the wagon, Miss Fletcher.'

Jeremiah was standing in the shelter of the archway outside the kitchen doorway. Wrapped in an old coachman's coat, which was at least a size too big for him, and knee breeches, he shook with fear, but he still carried the baby in his arms.

'Where are you taking the child so late at night? It'll catch its death,' Annie asked and pulled her shawl over her nightdress.

She had heard the movements from her bedroom window above the kitchen and had come to see what all the fuss was about. Annie felt a sense of panic rise within her. The more Jeremiah hesitated, the greater her fear for her friend rose. She had wanted to spend the evening with her father but did not know what to do for her friend. Their heads turned as they saw the wagon leaving the stables and crossing the coach yard.

'You best be gone, miss. If Amos sees you, there'll be trouble, I'm sure.'

Jeremiah avoided her eyes, which

made Annie feel sick. Whatever they were doing was not right, of that Annie Fletcher was sure. Surely Lady Constance was not capable of cold-blooded murder? She wasn't, though. She was ordering poor souls like Jeremiah, who had no choice but to obey, to do her dirty work for her.

If she was right, then how would she ever feel safe again? She knew too much. Her plans to escape Constance's grip had just been given a huge push forwards. Soon she would leave the hall and Father would be strong enough to work their small piece of land and return to his old position on the estate. If Lady Constance wanted to blame this on anyone, Annie realised she and Jeremiah would be her first choice.

She kissed the baby's cheek and stepped back into the shadow of the kitchen doorway, but issued the boy a threat.

'You look after that bairn, boy, or the hex will be on you.'

She hurried inside as Jeremiah

climbed aboard the wagon next to Amos Kell, the gamekeeper. Amos's scarred face turned to Jeremiah then stared at the child.

'You broody or summut?'

His coarse voice caused the baby to stir.

'Keep it quiet or I'll break its neck right here!' he snarled.

He led the wagon down the long drive to the iron gates from where two large stone lions peered proudly out into the dark night. Jeremiah sheltered the baby's face from the ice cold of the mist. The gloom crept up around them and a low mist clung to the ground.

The road took them away from the moor, down a wooded embankment then followed the sweep of the river. The moon's silvery light appeared to shimmer in the mist. The wagon followed the course of the old road by the riverbank. Large oak and willow were silhouetted in black against the moonlight.

In the back of the wagon lay the

motionless body of Georgette Davey. Jeremiah glanced back and saw two shovels thrown in at her side. He swallowed hard. Looking at the child, he realised that even without Fletcher's threat he could not be a party to her murder. Amos pulled the wagon off the road into a tree-covered clearing. The moon's light cut out. There was nothing but darkness and the mist surrounding them.

Back at the hall, Annie wrapped her cloak around her and headed off through the grounds. If she was quick, she could head off the wagon by the abbey. She had to follow them. Georgette's only means of escape was if she, Annie, could get to their destination in time. But Annie knew this was a dangerous night to be about late.

There was a night trade that was carried out around the hall. Her father had told her many times to stay in and not look out if she heard any strange noises.

There was a deathly silence broken

only by the light rustle of wind through the trees and the steady flow of the river's perpetual motion. The abbey's stone walls once doused in praise were losing the fight of the ravage of time as they crumbled, encased within the undergrowth. The air was still. The horse snorted and as Annie stumbled through bracken and over ruined stones of a long-gone age, she saw the wagon turn off the road into the thick of the grounds. Amos dismounted.

Annie ran faster and faster until she reached the ditch at the side of the ancient road. The wagon was pulled out of sight along the muddy track. Bending low, she crossed the road and followed the wagon's progress until it stopped amongst the forest's cover. Her breath escaped her in shimmering gasps as it met the cold night air. Somewhere an owl hooted and she prayed.

'Come lad, tha's got some diggin' to do, so best start soonest.'

She heard Amos's rough voice carry on the still night air. Jeremiah climbed down, still holding the child in one arm. Amos was lifting Georgette out of the back of the wagon. It was all Annie could do to stop herself shouting out.

'She dead, Mister Amos?' Jeremiah asked as he picked up the shovel with his free hand.

Annie held her chest, waiting for the answer.

'Not yet, lad, but soon. Put the brat down and dig.'

Amos started to dig, but Jeremiah hesitated then carefully placed the child next to its mother, carefully wrapping Georgette's arm around it. To Annie's delight and surprise, the woman's eyes opened fleetingly and she hugged her baby weakly, but reassuringly to her.

'Dig, you lazy heathen!' Amos yelled.

Annie moved slowly around the shadows.

'Yes, Mister Amos,' Jeremiah answered and once again Georgette's eyes flickered open, her mouth forming one silent word, 'Help!' Annie could see her clearly. She'd wrapped her shawl around her face so as not to reflect any light from either the moon's rays or Amos's lamp.

Jeremiah held his shovel in his hand and was about to start digging when he stopped and stared towards the old ruins. Annie looked and saw something move in the depth of the shadows. Jeremiah's head shot around. Between the old arches of the ivy-clad fallen parapets, moving smoothly through the midst, was the figure of a monk, the white habit covered only by a brown hooded cape. Amos looked to see what had caught Jeremiah's attention.

'Souls of monks, long gone. You heathen, dig!'

Amos looked to the boy. Both Annie and Jeremiah watched the monk disappear once more into the forest. The boy's mouth hung open as the shovel fell from his hand.

'You fool, they've now't to do with you. You stay out of their way and they'll stay out of yours. Them is as much livin' as you and me. So keep your head down and say and see nothin'! Here, stick the brat in there.'

Amos pointed to the small hole he had made in the ground. He strode over to Georgette.

Annie was about to launch herself at him when, without thinking of the consequences, Jeremiah lifted the shovel and cracked it down on Amos's head. The man fell to the ground, a trickle of blood running down by his temple.

Annie ran over to Georgette and had to duck quickly as Jeremiah nearly swung the spade at her, being scared out of his wits. Georgette tried to sit up. Her head felt heavy, but she looked at Jeremiah and saw the fear in his face as he dragged Amos's body into the cover of the wagon.

The baby started to cry loudly. Annie cradled it to her and Georgette stumbled but managed to rise to her feet. She wanted to pick up her child, and after a few attempts, managed to hold her.

'What to do now?' Annie muttered and looked first at Jeremiah and then towards the hidden body of Amos.

'I knows what to do with him,' Jeremiah answered. 'But you'll not see me again. I wish you well, missy, both of you, but I've got to run, and fast.'

Annie nodded, and said, 'God be with you, Jeremiah.'

A gunshot suddenly ripped through the trees, scaring the horse. It reared. Jeremiah jumped into the back of the wagon as the horse bolted. Georgette fell to her knees and as the spooked horse took off with the wagon, Annie saw that the boy had climbed to the front board and was fighting to regain control of the scared animal. He would not return. They had seen the last of Jeremiah, and, thank goodness, Amos Kell.

5

As Georgette sank to her knees, Annie felt the strength of an arm around her as she struggled to support both the girl and the baby, powerless to stop the nightmare that her life had become, with no energy to run along the road after Jeremiah and the wagon. She turned to plead with the figure who held her firmly in his grip.

The figure dressed as a monk forced her to the ground and whispered, 'Get out of here. Go to the road. Make haste!'

Annie could see the draped figures approaching through the darkness. The two women scurried down the path to the road, Annie supporting the exhausted Georgette, the baby, hugged closely, nestled and asleep, blissfully unaware of the danger it was in. Other white-clad figures were walking towards them through the ruins.

Annie glanced back and could see that the man who had let them pass was walking to meet the others. She swallowed, scared, but helped Georgette to walk to the road. Georgette, near to tears and in her dazed state, looked at her friend.

'What do we do now? Who are they?'

Annie watched the visions of a yesteryear move back into the forest. They carried burdens and moved steadily. She looked at her friend who stood, ruined, like the once great abbey, once so proud, so vibrant and alive, now with an uncertain future to be determined only, it seemed, by the will of God.

'First, to my father's cottage. We'll get you warm and the baby tended. Then I'll have to see what is happening at the hall. You must stay hidden. We must be swift.'

It took them an hour to reach the path to her old home. Georgette kept stumbling. Anne was scared for her. She felt cold, too cold.

A carriage thundered along the road behind them. There was no time to hide and no energy to run. It stopped just ahead of them and the door was opened. A well-dressed man stepped out. He approached the two frightened women.

'What on earth are two creatures such as you about on a night such as this?'

'My cousin lost her way. I have been out looking for her, but the hour is late now and we are cold and tired.'

Annie looked down, trying to be humble, and, hopefully, believable.

'Where do you go?' he asked looking apprehensively.

'My father's cottage, sir,' Annie answered, wishing he would just go away.

Georgette slumped to the ground, fainting. Annie held the child and the man tried to break her fall. The stranger's servant ran to his master.

'Carry this woman into the carriage. Woman, bring the baby. We'll take you where you can get help.'

'No, that . . . ' Annie began to speak, but the man looked at her sternly.

'Speak not and be grateful!'

'Yes, sir.'

Annie did not know what else to say or do.

'Pull the rug about you, Frederick, and sleep,' the man addressed a scrawny-looking youth who was huddled in the corner of the carriage. 'We shall be home before you wake.'

He helped the servant carry Georgette into the carriage, nestling her on the floor and covering her with a blanket. Annie and the baby sat opposite the youth, then the man entered, sitting next to the boy.

Annie saw the handle of a pistol inside his greatcoat as he bent over to check Georgette. She knew he had two well-armed men riding a-top the carriage. Frederick's face resumed a sulky expression as he pulled the blanket around his wiry frame.

'I want to get home, Father. It is not

safe to be out so late! It's a trap, a trap!' Frederick shouted, his whole countenance filled with fear. 'We're to die!'

'Hold your tongue, boy!' The man's rebuke was sharp and ill-tempered.

Frederick's sulky countenance intensified. He had started to shiver involuntarily. Annie could see he really was in fear of his life, but the man remained silent, staring out into the night as the coach descended into the valley. He placed his hand on the pistol, as if comforted by it. He seemed well aware of the gangs of smugglers who carried on their illicit business under the cover of darkness. Annie wondered whether to speak when the baby started to cry. She tried to comfort it.

However, tonight had a natural bright lunar light, so perhaps their journey would have no more interruptions. The coach increased speed. The man had given instructions to move as swiftly and as safely as possible. The coat-of-arms on the coach should be enough to warn off any ne'er-do-wells, she thought, but who could predict the reactions of such low lives? Suddenly, and with a shuddering jolt, the coach came to an abrupt halt.

'What is it, Benjamin?' the man asked his servant up top, and placed a comforting hand on top of Frederick's knee as the boy squealed out in fear and squirmed whilst hanging on tightly to the blanket.

'A wagon across the road, sir,' the liveryman shouted back.

'Approach carefully. If it is innocent, then move it swiftly and let us be on our way.'

Benjamin stepped down and in his great coat and hat, his large frame took on gigantuan proportions as the bright silvery moonlight silhouetted him. He leaned into the wagon carefully, and came back to the carriage, all the time looking around him cautiously.

'An accident, milord! The man is dead and the horse stolen or bolted.'

'Do you recognise him?' the man asked.

'I think he may be from Hallam Hall.

Looks like the gamekeeper.'

'Move the wagon. We'll send word to the hall. If it's murder then they'll have to sort the blackguards out once and for all.'

'I think not, sir. He smells badly of drink. Looks like an accident, milord,' Benjamin answered.

'Can you move the wagon?'

'Yes, milord.'

Annie stared at the baby.

'Do you know anything of this, miss?'

'He was giving my cousin a lift, but she ran away because he was worse for drink. She could not know this was to happen,' Annie lied, but felt that it would make their situation slightly more believable.

His lordship looked at the small baby. Frederick shrank into the farthest corner of the coach.

'Move the wagon.'

Benjamin nodded and went about his duty.

'This child is not long born.'

His lordship pulled the blanket from

Frederick and wrapped the tiny baby in its warmth. The child ceased to cry and settled down in Annie's arms once more.

'Take it to the poorhouse or the asylum before we catch something from it, Father,' Frederick cried out and tried to tug the blanket back.

The man glared at him reproachfully and Frederick folded his arms defiantly.

'This child may not survive without its poor mama, who herself looks not long for this world.'

Annie gasped at his words. Georgette must live. What would she do without her to tend the baby?

'However, it has been placed in my path and by every means that I can, I shall try to save it and the sad creature who birthed it.'

He looked compassionately at Annie.

'There is no sign of anyone else. We really should continue, sir. Williams has seen movements,' Benjamin said and looked agitated and anxious to continue the journey.

'Then go in haste. Take us to Speer. We shall see to our mercy errand before we return to the manor. They will need nourishment and warmth.'

He looked at all three of them and shook his head.

'No woman should be out on a night such as this. Have you no knowledge of the dangers that await a God-fearing soul around these parts?'

'We had little choice.' Annie kept her eyes on the child.

'Perhaps if you will not tell me more, then the good doctor may persuade you to be a little more forthcoming.'

The coach moved and with a crack of a whip continued along the sweeping road by the abbey ruins. It struggled up the steep climb on to the open moor road and the village beyond. Annie did not speak, not wishing to lie any more than she already had.

'What name does the child have, miss?'

'Bethany, my lord,' Annie replied, still staring at her friend's motionless form on the carriage floor.

'A girl child.'

Lord Edgar looked down at the tiny sleeping face, smiled and glanced towards Frederick. His lordship seemed pleased with himself that he had been so called to help this scrap of humanity. But all they saw on Frederick's face was a supercilious expression, as if there were a distasteful odour in the carriage with him.

The wheels turned with greater speed with such noise and haste that the scream that rang out into the night faded away into the woodland, unheard.

6

The carriage stopped outside the cottage on the outskirts of Beckton. Annie wanted the kindly stranger to take them straight to her father's home but Georgette desperately needed help. Benjamin opened the carriage door and lowered the step. Frederick glared at Annie as she climbed down carefully, with the baby held protectively in her arms.

Benjamin bent over the motionless figure inside the carriage, and lifted Georgette carefully over his shoulder. In the moonlight, her face looked almost waxen. Georgette desperately needed Samuel Speer's help and Annie could not do anything but follow their destiny and hope, prayerfully, they would survive. Looking down at the face of the tiny child she held, she wanted all three of them to come through this nightmare and be strong again.

When the door was opened, a tall figure greeted them, dressed in boots, breeches and a loose white shirt hanging freely about his hips. His ruffled hair and dishevelled appearance changed Dr Speer's appearance considerably. His eyes fell upon Georgette's listless form. Without hesitation he turned around and said, 'Bring her in here.'

He asked for no explanation but led them to the end of the cottage where there was a bed, chair and table with a water bowl and his bag.

'Place her on the bed, carefully.'

Benjamin obeyed and then stepped back, returning to the carriage and the petulant boy inside.

Annie followed the doctor, still embracing the new-born child.

'What happened, Edgar?'

Dr Speer addressed the stranger in a familiar tone. Annie realised they were well acquainted by their easy manner.

'We found these waifs by the abbey road. Can I leave them in your trusting care, Samuel? I have Frederick to return to his school. We should have been through here hours ago if the coach had not split its wheel outside Selby.'

Speer looked at Edgar and nodded.

'I'll take it from here.'

He looked at Annie sympathetically and took the baby from her.

'Thank you . . . er . . . ?'

Annie hesitated as she realised she had no idea who the kindly stranger was, other than he was obviously a man of position.

'Lord Carrington,' the man answered, then asked, 'Miss . . . ?'

'Thank you for your kindness, Lord Carrington.'

Annie stared at her friend who lay motionless on the bed, her breathing shallow.

'Fetch a bowl of warm water from the stove, miss,' Speer ordered Annie and she left them to find the stove at the other end of the cottage.

'Is all well, Edgar?' Annie heard the doctor ask.

'As can be. I must go and see to Frederick. I hope you can save the wench and find out what the truth is in this affair.'

He shook the hand of Speer and took his leave. The doctor addressed Annie as soon as they were alone.

'Place the bowl on the floor here and undress her whilst I examine the baby.'

He placed the child on the bed. The baby wailed as he unwrapped the cloth from its tiny, wriggling body.

'Her eyes opened,' Annie said, as she struggled to remove Georgette's soiled garments.

'A baby's cry is the strongest call a mother's brain can have. A special bond exists between them, reaching deeper than any other sound. Nature is a wonderful thing, when not abused. This little scrap of humanity may be small, but she is strong.'

For the next few hours, Annie

followed his every instruction as mother and child were cleaned and fed with warmed milk and nestled into each other. Georgette drifted in and out of consciousness. Both were weak. Both had a slight fever, but Annie did not doubt that they were in the best hands possible to save them. Samuel Speer worked tirelessly at his task until he was satisfied they both had a fighting chance.

Annie tidied up all the clothes and cloths then changed the water and saw to fetching new from the well. She heated it and ran back and forth between the bedroom and the stove as needed. Weary and driven only by their need, she worked without stopping. Modesty and propriety had no place here. Survival of her friend and her child was all that mattered.

When, finally, they had done all that they could, the doctor placed an arm across Annie's shoulders and walked her to the two chairs that graced either side of the stove. He poured her a warm drink. When she sipped it, the brandy that had been poured into it hit her taste buds hard, but she savoured each sip.

'What is your name? You did not give it the day I called at your cottage.'

He sat opposite her, in a casual manner, also drinking. He looked weary and dishevelled, and Annie could not help but find him attractive. More than his physical appearance, his caring nature and knowledge appealed to her greatly. She had mainly met men who were unschooled and worked on the land. Samuel Speer was very different.

'Annie.' She said no more, and sipped her drink as he nodded to Georgette.

'Who is she?'

He watched her closely as if analysing her reactions and answers.

'My cousin, Georgette. She tried to make her way to my father's cottage.'

Annie stared at the fire. She did not want to lie. Part of her was desperate to tell this newcomer to the village the absolute truth. But how could she? It was more farcical than anyone could believe — a lady had instructed her servants to murder the illegitimate child of their ex-governess and her husband. How could she possibly expect a doctor, a man of honour and integrity, to believe a servant's word against that of Lady Constance?

'Your cousin?' he repeated.

'Yes.'

Annie looked back at him sombrely, hoping he would believe her or at least let her lie stand.

'Married?'

'She was. Her husband died in the war.'

Lies, more lies, she thought. God forgive me. Annie felt as though she was burying herself in deceit but what could she do?

'In the morning, I shall ride and tell your father that you are all safe and well here, until she can return.'

He leaned forward, resting his elbows on his knees and looked straight into her eyes as she quickly responded.

‘No! That won’t be necessary. I mean, I’ll go. It will be a shock to him. I can return within the hour. It is not necessary for you to go. Georgette and the baby need you here.’

Annie looked at him, almost pleading inside. ‘You have been more than kindness itself to us. We cannot ask any more of you.’

‘You have not asked, Annie. I have gladly offered. Now you must sleep in my bed tonight.’

He stood up and grinned at the shocked expression that crossed Annie’s face.

‘I could not. It would not be proper. I shall sleep in the chair here,’ Annie protested, but warm and tired, she yearned for a soft bed on which to collapse.

‘You will do as I say. I have two patients to attend to. It will be a long night. You sleep soundly. I shall wake you in the morning and we shall discuss who is going to relate this story to your father then.’

He smiled in an almost knowing way.

She wondered if her lies were so transparent. If they were, what on earth would he be thinking of?

'Good-night, Annie.'

He held out a hand to her and she rose to her feet. He did not let go of hers and she followed him, led like a child to his own four-poster bed. Clean linen sheets and sumptuous blankets lay upon it.

'Sleep well.'

He left her and closed the shutter doors that turned the corner of the cottage into a private chamber. She heard him walk on the stone floor back towards Georgette. She knew he did not believe her story, she knew that. But then she asked herself, why should he? She had lied repeatedly to him. In her heart she realised that she wished it could be different, but this was not just her life. Georgette's and Bethany's depended on the web of deceit she wove. They would not survive the poorhouse, of that Annie was sure.

Honesty had been betrayed and it

bothered Annie that the man whose bed she now lay on knew her only as a false woman. She hugged the pillow to her, breathed in his scent as she drifted into a blissful sleep.

* * *

Next day, Samuel Speer tethered his horse and trap outside the cottage of Thomas Haswell, Annie's father. He knocked on the door and was delighted when Thomas himself opened it.

'Good morning, Doctor Speer. This is an early surprise. Would you join me in a drink?'

Thomas stepped back inviting him inside.

'I would love to.'

Samuel shook his patient's hand with a warm greeting. He liked Thomas and, he admitted to himself, his daughter. The latter, though, was not telling him the truth, that much he could sense, but the reasons for the girl's lies were not clear to him. Yet, his instincts assured him she was, in essence, trustworthy, so what was the mystery of two respectable women and a baby out at such a late hour in an inhospitable and dangerous place?

Both men sat down, one at either side of the warm hearth, warming themselves by the fire. Thomas placed a tankard in Samuel's hand and poured ale from a pewter jug.

'Not too much, Thomas. It is early and I have patients to attend to. Have your headaches stopped now?' he asked, and saw the smile of relief on Thomas's face that gave him his answer.

'I could tell you what I would like to do to Dr Brown, but I suppose I would have to join the end of a very long queue. God will deal with him when his time comes, I have no doubt.'

Thomas looked down at his hands thoughtfully.

'At least I can say that now with a degree of honesty.'

'Why do you say that? Are you not a man of faith?'

Samuel realised Thomas was not the usual kind of farmhand. He spoke properly, with education and thought. Both father and daughter intrigued him.

'I was a minister who spoke too openly, criticising the church and establishment for letting down the bulk of God's children. I ruffled feathers, rocked too many boats and lost my position. The change in lifestyle, I am sure, led to the early demise of my lovely wife. Yes, I am a man of faith, sir, but that faith has been sorely tested.'

'Brown's judgement with his maker may come early as he has been arrested for the murder of a widow who left her estate to him. Her son was suspicious of his methods and motives.'

Samuel watched as Thomas shook his head.

'Perhaps I am lucky that I am not a rich man or he may have had more than a drug in my elixir. Now tell me, it is only two days since you were here and told me I was fit to start doing some work again, so what brings you here so early in the morning?'

'Annie,' Samuel began. 'She works very hard.'

Samuel wished he had chosen different words as they appeared to pierce Thomas like a knife.

'I wish it had been different. She is clever, educated, but she works all the hours God sends for that woman over at the hall. Sorry, I do not mean to be ungrateful or disrespectful but Lady Constance Hallam is . . . '

Thomas faltered as he sought for the correct words.

'A demanding lady?' Samuel offered.

'Yes, that's it. Annie doesn't get home most nights because she has to be on call. It will be different soon, you'll see. I'll whip this land into shape and I'll be at the hall for work next week.'

Thomas raised his head proudly as he spoke.

'Take care not to do too much too soon, Thomas.' Samuel shifted slightly in his chair. 'Were you expecting her here last night?'

'Annie, you mean? No. Why do you ask?'

'Does she have a cousin or anyone who could help out here?'

Samuel's question appeared to surprise Thomas. The man was obviously grateful to him for saving him from a dormant life, but people in these parts were wary of strangers and in particular ones who asked personal questions.

'Why should she need help here? I am fit now and soon she will be back here where she belongs. Then she can do what she is gifted at,' Thomas looked at Samuel proudly, 'teach.'

The door burst open at that moment and Annie arrived, flushed, looking as though she had been running. Samuel rose to his feet and offered her his chair.

'Is everything all right, Father?' she asked and gave him a quick hug.

'Yes.' He paused glancing at Samuel. 'I think so.'

'What brings you here at this hour?' Thomas asked.

‘I must return to the hall soon, but I just wanted to check on you first,’ Annie said, but in her panic of realising that the doctor could have spoken to her father already about Georgette, had not thought carefully about her words.

She had to return to the hall in order that Lady Constance had no knowledge of what had happened to Georgette or the baby. He must not be suspicious of her. Everything seemed a total mess and Annie was somehow caught up in the middle of it.

‘What do you mean return to the hall? Where have you been all night?’ Thomas demanded and his face showed his annoyance and concern.

Annie opened her mouth to speak, but Samuel Speer’s words cut across hers.

‘I did not want to worry you, Thomas, but Annie came to see me last night, concerned about the state of her relative. Her fatigue was so great that she fell sound asleep. It was my medical opinion that she would do best to stay where she was. I came here to explain what had happened and tell you she was perfectly safe.'

Annie stared at the handsome man before her, realising that he had neither lied, nor told the exact truth. He had said Annie was concerned about her relative, without naming Georgette, and that she had fallen asleep in his bed. A wave of emotion swept through her at the thought of it. What would her father have said had he known? Yet Dr Speer had made it sound innocent, necessary in some way.

'That is very kind of you, Doctor. However, Annie should know better than to walk these parts at night.'

Annie did not meet her father's glare for he knew only too well about the trade, the contraband that was shifted through the abbey grounds on certain nights of the month.

'The weather was not so severe last night, but it is ill advised for a young woman to venture out on a night alone, no matter how noble the reason.'

Dr Speer had his back to her father. He surprised her with a broad grin. She did not quite know what to make of it.

'Doctor, you are a stranger around here,' Thomas said. 'I understand and appreciate your good intentions, but may I advise you, also, to be careful where your feet take you after the hours of darkness. The abbey is renowned for the strange sightings of monks that walk within its ruins.'

Samuel turned to face him.

'I am a man of science. I do not fear ghosts or the dead.'

'Perhaps not, but you would be a wise man if you were careful of whom, amongst the living, you crossed in these parts. I'll say no more as I may have said too much already, but I owe you, lad. Please, heed my words.'

Thomas offered his hand in friendship. The doctor shook it.

'I will.'

'I must go to the hall, Father.' Annie smiled warmly at him. 'You look so well.' Annie hugged him once more.

'I shall drop you there, Miss Annie.'

Speer made it sound as if it were not an offer but an instruction.

'You be off, lass. Muriel will pop in shortly and then we're goin' to start some work on the place. I've been idle long enough.'

Annie smiled although that familiar pang of jealousy rose within her when Muriel's name was mentioned. The woman seemed to be increasing her visits to her father. Annie only knew her as a new neighbour, recently moved to the village. She was a stranger, like the good doctor, therefore an unknown.

However, she followed the kindly doctor out of the cottage and climbed on to his carriage.

The horse was driven steadily, even slowly towards the hall. For a while, neither spoke, then when out of view of the cottage, the doctor looked at her.

'Well?'

'I'm a bit tired but I feel greatly

relieved to see Georgette and the baby sleeping soundly in warm beds this morning.'

Annie looked across the purple moorland in the distance before they approached the shelter of the trees. Beckton lay in its own hidden dale, a cluster of stone cottages along one broad street, St Cuthbert's church dominating the village at its southernmost point.

'I am no fool, neither are you,' Dr Speer said. 'Who is Georgette, who fathered her child and what is her situation, other than fairly desperate from all that I have seen? She clearly is no cousin of yours.'

He stopped the trap and waited for Annie to reply.

'The baby is hers, I assure you.'

Annie was flustered. If she told more lies, he might take Georgette to the poorhouse or the magistrates. If she told him the truth, she might be sent to the asylum herself for making what would surely sound to him, as indeed it did to her own ears, such a fanciful tale.

'I don't need to be a doctor, Annie, to have figured out that much. You are protecting a friend, are you not?'

She looked at him. His dark eyes appeared almost to stare at hers in total understanding. Yet how could he possibly comprehend what was going on?

'Yes,' she answered somewhat hesitantly.

'A fallen friend?'

He tilted his head slightly, watching her every gesture.

'Yes, but she had been treated badly. I mean, abandoned. She needs protection from a more powerful man.'

'We shall return to my cottage. You have a lot to tell me, Annie, and I intend to listen to every word.'

He flicked the horse's rump with its reins.

'No, I must go to the hall.' She gripped his arm. 'I really must.'

'Then you must promise to return to me later today. Promise me.'

'I will.'

Annie swallowed hard. There seemed no other choice. But what could she honestly tell him that would not endanger both herself and Georgette?

7

Lady Constance summoned Jeremiah to the library. She was vexed and surprised that the youth had not reported to her first thing to confirm that the night's work had been done successfully. After waiting some ten minutes, there was an ineffectual knock on the door. It had fallen upon the shoulders of a young maid called Millie to tell her he could not be found.

'Where is the young fool?' Lady Constance shouted at the poor, trembling girl.

'No-one knows, milady. We've looked everywhere. His bed's not been slept in. Mister Amos has not turned up at the stables this mornin' either. There's a wagon missin', too, milady.'

Millie's voice became more confident and quickened in pace once she started to divulge the morning's mysterious events to her mistress.

'Send Jenkins out to fetch Mr McGregor, the customs man, from the coastguards at Whitby. Tell him we have two servants and a wagon missing and ask him to inform me if he might know something of their whereabouts.'

Lady Constance stared as the simple-minded Millie scurried towards the door. Constance grinned at the foolish child.

'Millicent!' she snapped the word out and watched as the girl's face paled with fear.

'Yes, milady.'

Her voice was almost inaudible as she awaited Constance's next command or rebuke. Lady Constance mellowed her voice.

'Tell Cook I wish to see her immediately.'

'Yes, milady.'

Millie nodded and almost ran from the room.

As Millie left, Lady Constance stared at the ornate fireplace.

'Damnation!' she said, and felt as though she would throw the Wedgwood vase which adorned it crashing into the hearth, but that would be folly.

If the buffoons had not carried out such a simple task without messing it up, then everything at the hall had to be as normal as could be. No suspicion should fall on to her or Lord Hallam. But where were Georgette and the brat? Had Amos done what she ordered or taken her to sell at market?

She'd heard of such things. Perhaps Amos had got greedy and decided to sell them and Jeremiah, too, and make off with the proceeds. So long as she never heard from them again, why should she care?

It was with a great deal of trepidation that Cook approached the door. She was never summoned to her ladyship unless there was a party, ball or function in the offing. There wasn't, not for another month, so that meant one thing — trouble.

Lady Constance had seated herself

by the fire. She smoothed her silk gown and waited a moment to compose herself before her servant arrived. Constance liked silk. It was her favourite fabric. It looked delicate, felt smooth but had great strength if you knew how to use it, like she did. She liked her servants to fret a little before they came into her presence. It made her dealings with them far more entertaining.

'Enter.'

Constance folded her hands loosely on her lap, and watched the rosy-cheeked Cook enter the room and bob a clumsy curtsey before her.

'You wanted to see me, milady?' Cook said and smiled broadly at her.

'Obviously,' Constance replied curtly, but noticed that the woman did not flinch at her tone, unlike Millie.

She would have to apply a different tactic with her. She had worked at the estate for years and knew a great deal, no doubt, about everything that went on there.

'Where is Amos?' Constance asked the woman, who shrugged her shoulders.

'I've no idea. He was there for 'is supper last night and went off as usual. This mornin', Jeremiah did not come in for 'is food and Amos ne'er showed. I sent Millie over to the stables to find 'im, Jeremiah, that is, and he was nowhere to be found.'

'A wagon is missing. Did you hear them take it out last night?'

Lady Constance watched as the Cook shook her head.

'Sorry, milady, I sleeps like a log. I don't hear nothin' once I'm off until I rise in the mornin'.' Cook looked open-eyed at her mistress.

Lady Constance couldn't tell if she was lying or not, which was extremely annoying.

'My eggs were not fresh enough this morning. I expect better of you than that.'

Constance saw Cook's cheeks flush even more red than their normal hue. It pleased her, because everyone had their weakness, pride was one such, and now she knew what Cook's was.

'They was fresh when they left my kitchen, milady,' Cook said in a hurt tone.

'Then I should chastise Millie. The lazy girl must have dallied with my tray.'

Alarm registered on Cook's face. So how loyal would she be to her fellow staff?

'Send her back here when you return,' Constance said.

'I don't think that will be necessary, milady. I'll make sure they are fresh as can be tomorrow.'

Cook obviously found it hard to say the words, but she had swallowed her pride to protect Millie. Constance knew instantly the woman would not divulge anything she did or did not know to her.

'Send Annie up to me. That will be all.'

Constance dismissed her with a gesture of the hand. If she could find a replacement of her own choice for her, she surely would. But this was not London, and she had to put up with peasants, for now. But soon, life would be very different. Lady Constance had plans for a brighter future.

* * *

Dr Speer wanted to take Annie up the driveway to the hall and leave her almost at its door, but Annie would not have it. She alighted at the boundary of Hallam's grounds, nearest to the kitchens.

'Thank you, sir.'

She looked up at the handsome figure who sat calmly, smiling back at her. Her hand still rested on the seat. He took it in his.

'You are a mystery, Annie. I shall know the truth today, please, no matter what it is. I have two patients under my roof. I cannot help them or you, unless I understand what is happening here.'

He kissed the back of her hand. She

did not know if he were playing with her or if it was a natural response. Annie nodded and withdrew her hand quickly.

'I must go.'

His touch, his very presence, made her feel a growing warmth inside. Yet he was a professional man and she a maid. What did he know of her or her past? To him she was merely a servant, one who had foolishly displayed herself to him in the cottage, and lied to him under his own roof, even sleeping in his own bed. He could only think her loose and of poor character. She was being foolish.

Annie entered the kitchens, deep in thought.

'The cheeky bitch!'

Cook's outburst as she appeared from the servants' stairs, full of fury, made Annie run straight over to her.

'What has happened?' Annie asked as Cook rolled her sleeves up in temper.

Whenever something really upset her, she would do that then start making bread dough. That dough was in for a pounding this morning as Annie had never seen her so irate.

'My eggs are always perfect . . . the stuck-up piece of . . .'

'Cook, what is happening?' Annie shouted over her outrage in order to make herself heard.

'She criticised my eggs. Can you believe that? And she did it on purpose! You must go up and see her but do somethin' with your hair first.'

Annie tried to tidy herself up. Cook watched her.

'Amos, Jeremiah and a wagon have gone.'

Annie looked at her, surprised.

'Really?'

'Wipe the mud off yer boots, woman.' Cook gave her an old damp rag. 'What's goin' on, Annie? Don't tell me you're not in more trouble than just your sick pa.'

Cook waved a fat index finger at her.

'He's much better now. Did you hear about Dr Brown?' Annie tried to sidetrack her whilst she wiped the last evidence of mud from her shoes.

'He's bin askin' for trouble for years, that man. But what's goin' on 'ere?'

'Cook, I've got to go to Lady Constance. There'll be trouble if I don't.'

She kissed the older woman on her cheek and ran up the stairs. She was going to spend a lot of time explaining many things to a lot of people, but not until she was sure Georgette and the baby were safe.

8

'You wanted to see me, milady?' Annie entered the room where Lady Constance was standing in an agitated fashion by the great fireplace. The pale lemon silk gown she wore contrasted with her dark hair and, Annie reflected, her similarly dark nature.

'Do not flatter yourself, woman.' She faced Annie directly. 'Close the door and approach.'

Annie did as she was ordered. She came within three feet of her mistress. Lady Constance was facing the fire as if mesmerised by the flames as they danced across the coals.

'What do you know of the events that took place last night, Fletcher?'

Her eyes focused on her face with an intense and piercing stare, but Annie was not like Millie, scared of her own shadow. No, Annie looked boldly and blankly back.

'Know what, milady? I was a-bed, fast asleep.' Annie kept a calm composure.

'Whose bed was that?' Lady Constance sneered.

Annie felt a pang of guilt as if Lady Constance's wit had inadvertently stumbled across a truth.

'You were not in your own!' Her voice was sharp and accusing.

Annie was not a person to gamble. However, she had always followed her intuition. Her father had given up his ministry but his teachings on gambling and other sinful acts had been thorough.

She had never, ever known Lady Constance to venture into the servants' quarters.

Something about the woman's manner told Annie she was in fact bluffing. Her plans had gone badly wrong. Annie realised Constance should not know how wrong, though. Besides, Cook would have warned Annie if Lady Constance had summoned her when she was absent.

Therefore, Annie lied confidently, sinning once more.

'But I was, milady.'

Lady Constance stared at her, as if trying to figure out if she were telling the truth.

'Go and check on your friend and see if she and the child need anything.'

Lady Constance watched her closely and Annie suddenly realised that she should not have any knowledge at all of the night's activities and therefore would still expect Georgette to be in her room.

'Yes, milady.'

Annie made her way to the door.

'Woman, do you really not know?' Lady Constance's voice rose slightly as if in disbelief.

Annie faced her.

'Know what, milady?'

She tried to look as concerned and confused as she could without overdoing her feigned concern.

'They are no more.'

Lady Constance's expression conveyed no feeling, no concern and no remorse.

The woman had a heart of stone.

'Where are Georgette and the baby, Lady Constance?'

Annie's face was flushed with indignation at the charade she was being forced to play out. It served to make her look shaken and concerned for her friend. Constance took in a sharp intake of breath and looked at Annie wide-eyed.

'My dear child, I was going to ask you the same question, as they are not in their room.'

She sniffed at a lace kerchief, as if holding back a sob, or even a tear. Placing one hand over her mouth, she sat down in the chair.

'I am to sort that whole mess out also. Yet, in the meantime, my servants are disappearing into the night. All this when Lord Hallam is away on business. How am I supposed to deal with such complicated events? Who is to tend the horses now that Amos and Jeremiah have deserted their posts? How selfish can people be?'

She stood up suddenly, facing Annie.

'If that ungrateful wretch has run away, I shall wash my hands of her and deny she was anything other than a loose woman who'd sleep with a common stable-hand. Yes, that is it! They must have eloped together. You must deny all knowledge of her if anyone asks any questions. She shall be declared delirious, possessed with evil demons.'

Lady Constance giggled like a naughty child then poked Annie's shoulder with her finger.

'Last night, Amos must have taken her and the child. You must have told him about her!'

'I did no such thing, Lady Constance. It has been a secret, as you said it must remain. I have not told a soul, upon my word. Who would believe me anyway?'

Annie looked at the evil woman before her. A manipulator of truth and people, she considered everyone to be no more than mere pawns in her latest quest for power.

'How is your father these days?'

The sudden change of subject surprised Annie but she tried not to show it.

'He is a little better,' Annie said cautiously.

'Good, I'm pleased to hear it. In case I no longer require your services here, it would be as well he is, for you are still three months behind in your rent. How sad it would be if he were to be thrown in the debtors' gaol when he was just starting to recover. I should be careful to whom you say what, Annie Fletcher.'

'Yes, milady.'

Annie dipped a curtsey. She wanted to slap her mistress across her smug face, but what could she do? What was she to tell Dr Speer? She had given her word that she would return and speak with him later that very day. If she trusted him and he turned to Lady Constance for proof of her story all would be lost.

A tap on the door interrupted their discussion.

'Who is it?' Lady Constance called in a vexed manner, her eyes still staring into Annie's.

'There is a Dr Speer to see you, milady.'

A card was brought to her on a silver salver.

'Does nobody have the grace to announce beforehand their intention to call appropriately any more?'

She looked at the card, then dismissed Annie with a flick of her wrist.

'For goodness' sake, woman, wash yourself and do something with that ghastly hair. It is an abomination. You smell worse than the pigs.'

Annie gritted her teeth and answered calmly, 'Yes, milady.'

'Show him in, Edwards.'

Annie left quietly, but as she saw Dr Speer approaching, she wanted to reach out to him and beg him not to speak of Georgette and the baby. Edwards walked into the room with the doctor following behind. In a moment of desperation she touched his sleeve as he drew level with her.

He stopped and looked down at her troubled face.

'Please, don't say . . . '

'This way, sir.'

Edwards had stepped back to find him. He looked curtly at Annie.

'About your business, Fletcher!'

She had to walk off, without finishing her plea. She heard Edwards' pompous voice apologising to him for her dishevelled appearance and lowly manners.

'She's a village girl, sir, lacking in social graces.'

Annie glanced back to see Speer enter the room. Her stomach constricted with worry. What was his business here, and would he betray Georgette without truly realising the danger the woman was in?

Only time would tell.

Annie returned to the kitchens feeling light-headed with all the worry.

She steadied herself on the back of a chair.

'Whatever is goin' on here, lass?'

Cook put her ample arm around her and sat her down by the open fire. She poured her a small glass of brandy from a bottle that she produced from underneath two logs at the back of the log pile by the fire. Annie looked on in amazement as she sipped the liquid, best brandy, smooth and warm.

'Whatever are you doing with this?' she asked, knowing it should be well beyond the purse of a servant. 'If his lordship finds out about it, having his best brandy, there'll be no mercy shown, Cook.'

'That's not from their cellar, lass. No, that is a present from Amos Kell for keeping my eyes, ears and mouth firm shut as to the comings and goings over at the stables. My room overlooks them, you know. If you're not aware of Amos's other work then you're a lot more foolish than I'd given you credit for, lass.'

Cook sat down opposite Annie, balancing her rump on a stool.

'So tell me what he was about last night? That weren't no normal run he was doin', was it?'

'If he's part of the local trade, why shouldn't it be, Cook?' Annie asked, as she sipped the warming fluid, savouring it as it calmed her tense nerves.

'Because I knew when he was supposed to go out, and he left early. They're supposed to keep to times, so there ain't any mistakes. He was angry and I had to swear not to even look out of my own window all evening and night, but I heard the wagon go. I heard voices. Sounded like Jeremiah and a woman first — you. Amos was edgy all day, and so was Jeremiah. No, there was summut else happening and you knows what it was, Annie Fletcher.'

Cook stared at her but Annie dared not say one word of the truth to her.

'Do you know where they are now?' Annie asked genuinely because she last saw Jeremiah taking Amos's body and the wagon off toward the moor, but the wagon had been discovered across the road with Amos in it.

'We wait to find out. I hope to God, Annie, what whatever that bitch has got you into, you can escape untarnished. Now, as I'm obviously wasting my time here, I've got much work to do.'

'Trust me, Cook. I wish I could reveal all I know to you, but my father is not able to pay the rent on the cottage yet. Gaol would kill him. He needs to build up his strength again. When he can, things will be different, you'll see.'

Annie smiled at her friend hoping she would understand.

'She's holding your arrears over you, isn't she?' Cook said angrily.

Annie nodded regretfully. They were so near being clear of this whole horrendous period in their lives that she only needed two more months then they would be free of their debts to the Hallam estates. If only she could sort out this nightmare without compromising Georgette's position further.

'Go freshen up. If she doesn't need you later, you may as well visit your father, and take him a pie.'

Cook patted Annie's back and she thanked her. Just then, Millie came bustling in, full of excitement.

'You'll never guess what has happened, Cook,' she blurted out, hardly able to contain herself.

'Unless you tell us, girl, I doubt we will,' Cook said dryly.

'I was cleanin' by the hallway and I heard a shriek from her ladyship. Well, I rushed in, as anyone would, with Mr Edwards, of course. I mean, she was in the room with a stranger, weren't she? Anyhow, turns out Amos Kell's body were found, dead, by the smashed-up wagon in the early hours of this morning. They reckon it were the work of Jeb Webb's gang what did it on a run! The dragoons have been told and the doctor's seen him.'

Millie's eyes were so wide she looked

like she would burst with all the gossip in her head.

'So what happened?' Annie asked.

She felt relief that this news at least provided a reason for Samuel Speer to call, but then she froze as she realised that if he told the whole truth, she, Georgette, Lord Carrington and his obnoxious son would all be involved and questioned as to the body's discovery.

'Well, Lady Constance came over all faint like. The doctor waved some smelly stuff under her nostrils and she rallied round. She was all of a fuss then asked if Jeremiah had been found with him. No, says the good doctor. The wagon was only found on the moors by accident when a coach came across it on its way to Whitby.'

'Whose coach?' Annie asked.

'The stagecoach. It arrives in Whitby early of a mornin'. Well, it would be delayed today, that's for sure.'

Millie was really enjoying herself. She loved gossip and this, Annie could tell, was the juiciest she had ever shared.

'Did you say he was found on the moor road?'

Annie queried the girl's tale but was acutely aware that Cook's eyes were fixed on her.

'Yes, Annie, up by the old cross. Do you think it was the ghost of a highwayman what spooked the horses? I've heard there's been sightings up there of ghostly riders of the night before now.'

'Foolish child! There's no ghosts but bad spirits about that's for sure and I don't mean dead 'uns!' Cook turned and stared pointedly at Annie. 'You best sort yourself out, girl, and double quick. It may be there'll be lots of folk asking lots of questions about this. Go sort yerself now!'

Cook's words were stern but Annie realised she was worried about her, so she agreed.

'Oh, Lady Constance asked for a tray to be sent up quick for her and the doctor, soonest.'

Millie smiled at Cook well pleased with herself and was taken aback with the response she received.

'You idiot, girl! Could you not have said that first before you rabbitted on about Amos?'

Cook slammed a silver tray down on the large oak table.

'Give me strength! Think, lass, what can be being done whilst you tittle-tattle and get on with it. No wonder you're forever in bother!'

Annie poured herself a bowl of warm water and carried it carefully to the little room she used at the hall. It was cramped but she washed and changed into her one other dress. She brushed out her hair and groomed herself. When she returned, fresh faced, she looked a much prettier person than the one who ascended the stairs, not that she was aware of her own natural beauty.

Millie was sulkily skinning hares by the old sink. Obviously her rebuke had been thorough. Cook was putting the finishing touches to the tray.

‘Annie, take this up there and don’t spill anything.’

‘Me?’

Cook rounded on her. Annie loved the woman but hated her rages when she was crossed. Before she had a chance to shout any more, Annie lifted the tray carefully and smiled at her.

‘Straightaway, Cook,’ she said.

Edwards raised an eyebrow at her when she appeared from the stairs into the hall.

‘Where is the girl, Millicent?’

His tone was abrupt. He had never liked Annie. She suspected it was because she had kept the secret of Georgette to herself. He liked to think he knew everything about everyone and the happenings at the hall.

‘Helping Cook. Would you like to take the tray in, Mr Edwards?’

Annie hoped he would say yes, but he merely announced its arrival and she had to walk steadily across the long room to place it on an inlaid marquetry table. Her eyes purposefully did not fall upon Samuel Speer.

'Fletcher.'

Lady Constance's voice made her shake inside. She hoped it was not visible to her eyes.

'Yes, milady.'

Annie couldn't help but catch Dr Speer's look as she faced her mistress. He seemed surprised by her appearance. Not surprising, she thought, as she must have appeared like a woman of the street, so shabby was she after running around all night.

'Have you met Dr Speer before?'

The question seemed to surprise him also, so Annie, who was now used to Lady Constance's games with people's minds, stayed calm.

'Why, yes, milady.'

'How so?'

Constance looked from one to the other as if such contact was highly unlikely.

'I would not have thought that a person of your rank could afford the services of a doctor of the University of

Edinburgh. Surely that Brown person would provide what necessary potions you required.'

'The doctor was kind enough to call in on my father,' Annie explained.

'You do charity work, Doctor Speer? How generous of you.' Lady Constance smiled sweetly at him.

Annie flushed with embarrassment. Yes, she was poor, but there was no need to make her feel so low in front of him.

'I was merely familiarising myself with the poorer families in the village to establish the state of the health of the community. It is a subject I have an interest in. Brown, however, would have had difficulty passing for a surgeon, let alone an apothecarist in a larger town.'

His voice did not disguise the genuine indignation he obviously felt by Brown's antics. The man had betrayed the very trust of those who believed in him and parted with their hard-earned cash. He was no better than the leeches the man had occasionally used on his patients, or should she call them victims, her father included. Dr Speer's words cut across her thoughts.

'Mr Fletcher will be well enough to return to work very soon,' Samuel said.

'Oh, good. My husband will be delighted. He has been so tolerant. It does not do to let one peasant off their rent whilst others still toil. They feel ill-treated, you understand. Annie here has done her best, but I need trained staff, not farmhands within my service. You understand, Doctor Speer, don't you?'

'Indeed, Lady Constance, I do.'

He smiled at her then, and as she sipped her tea, Samuel Speer winked at Annie.

'Well, Fletcher. What do you wait for, girl? Go about your chores.'

'Yes, milady.'

Annie dipped a quick curtsey and left.

Whatever they had discussed she did not think for one moment that it included Georgette, yet she felt the doctor knew more about events than he had given away. She had no idea what was happening around her, but decided she would wait her time to find out.

Two hours later, Lady Constance summoned her coach and, with Edwards travelling as an escort, left the hall. Annie immediately made her way to her father's cottage. She had to check on him first then she could concentrate on Georgette and find out what Dr Speer intended to do next.

As she approached her father's door she thought she heard the sound of laughter inside. Slowly she opened it and stepped in. She could not believe her own eyes. There, in an intimate embrace, were her father and the woman, Muriel! Annie slammed the door shut behind her as she ran off down the road. She heard his voice, his pitiful call to return so that he could explain.

No need, she thought, and it sickened her. Anger filled her at the sense of betrayal, furious at her own naïvety. Her life was a complete mess, but she was determined to save Georgette and the poor innocent Bethany.

9

Annie ran until she had no energy left. Her own father had betrayed her, the only person in the world she had left to her as kin, and he had fallen so far out of grace, that he was dallying with a village woman whilst she strove to keep a roof over his head.

Dr Brown had sold his soul for greed, her own father his for lust, Lady Constance for power. Was there nothing to protect the innocent from these people? Even she had lied, frequently, of late, but to save her innocent and naïve friend and the poor child. Surely she would be forgiven her indiscretion.

Part of her would always love her father. She always would, but once his debt to the estate was cleared she would never set eyes on him or that vile woman ever again, Annie vowed. He had betrayed her devotion and sullied the memory of her dear mother.

It was a good hour later before she had composed herself sufficiently to approach the gates of the doctor's cottage. She knocked on the door, and waited patiently. At first there was no sign of life, but then she heard a baby cry. Bethany! She knocked again. Still no reply came.

Annie skirted around the back of the cottage to where she found a small herb garden. She raised her skirts high and stepped over the low fence. Following the stone cottage wall, she knocked again, this time on the back door. When it opened slightly with her gentle knock, Annie looked around her but saw no-one.

She expected to see at least a day maid. Who cooked and cleaned for him? He was an educated man. He had standards to maintain. Yet, why should he stay in such a humble abode? She entered the cottage and tiptoed past the table and hearth, peering along the narrow corridor to the shuttered rooms from whence the baby's cry came. Annie made her way to the baby and hugged its carefully-wrapped body.

Georgette lay across the narrow corridor, fast asleep on the bed. Annie saw how waxen she looked. The baby settled, but Annie put her hand to Georgette's forehead. It was warm, but her breath seemed shallow.

'Do you normally let yourself into a stranger's house uninvited?'

The man's voice which broke the silence was deep and strangely familiar. Annie jumped nervously as Lord Carrington, dressed in a casual riding outfit with a caped cloak, stood leaning against the wall of the cottage.

'I knocked. I could hear the baby cry and I wanted to know how my cousin fared, sir.' Annie hugged the child. 'She looks so ill, sir.'

'She is. She lost much blood, but Samuel thinks she is strong and will pull through her ordeal. I pray it is so.'

Lord Carrington stared at the floor for a moment. He still carried a riding crop, which he used to flick at his boot. He looked like a man with much on his mind.

'Why did you call her your cousin?' He looked accusingly at her. 'She is no relative of yours, Miss Fletcher, of that I am certain.'

Annie was surprised by the tone of his voice.

'How do you know that? You choose to disbelieve me?'

She looked at him, guarding the baby protectively in her arms.

'Woman, I'm in no mood to play games. Samuel will return soon and then I want to know the whole story, everything that has passed between whoever defiled this beautiful, innocent creature.'

Annie thought hard for a moment. She could tell him the whole truth and whatever unfolded on her father would in some way be a vindictive gesture on her part. However, Annie was not vindictive and in this sad world she no longer knew whom to trust. Perhaps a total stranger offered her more trust than the people she had grown up with. Her world had turned upside down and everyone in it had in some way changed.

'I cannot say. Her future . . . ' She looked at Bethany. 'Their future lies in my hands. It is not for me to betray them. When Georgette awakes she will decide for herself what needs to be said.'

'Your motives are noble, but your judgement is lacking. I have already saved all three of your lives once. I am not about to toss any of you to the wolves. Trust me and tell me now!'

She shook her had.

'I don't think I will trust anyone ever again.'

She looked solemnly at Georgette.

'Annie, you are amongst friends here.'

Samuel's voice surprised her. He had obviously entered the back door also. He continued his story.

'This woman is not your cousin

because, my dear Annie, she is mine. I have searched for her since she stopped writing to me nearly two seasons since. I can now see why.'

He stroked the baby's cheeks.

'She was a governess at the hall, that I know. It was only a temporary arrangement whilst I finished my education and then we were to set up a home in Whitby. I would have my practice and Georgette was to set up a school for unfortunate children. I would tend their ills. We would hence give back to those less fortunate. Edgar, here, was tied up with business of his own. Once finished, he would return to his estate by the coast. However, events unfolded that changed things dramatically for all of us. Georgette seemed to vanish without trace.'

Samuel looked at the prone figure and Annie felt a pang of sadness because she saw something in his expression that made her realise he loved her. Perhaps they were to wed and Georgette's actions had scuppered her dreams. Annie swallowed. It made no sense to her but she almost felt jealous of the woman who fought for her life on the bed. At least she had something to fight for, two things — a beautiful child and a handsome man, a caring man, who obviously adored her. Annie looked at him and her heart told her how easy it would have been for her to do likewise.

'She was at the hall the whole time.'

Annie saw Lord Carrington grit his teeth and clench his fist at her reply.

'How so?'

Annie explained what had happened, how Lord Hallam had tricked and duped Georgette and then how Lady Constance had emotionally blackmailed her into a situation that was as intolerable as it was inescapable. When Annie finished, she watched both men with trepidation. Had she said too much?

Lord Carrington fell on one knee at the side of Georgette's bed. Samuel cupped Annie's elbow and walked her to the kitchen table.

'I don't understand. Shouldn't you be in there? I mean . . . ' Annie whispered to Samuel.

'She is safe. She is not the only one to have been played for a fool by Lady Constance. Lord Carrington and Georgette had plans to wed once we were respectably established in Whitby. However, events overtook him, Annie. It is best to leave him a moment. You must stay here. I've settled the outstanding rent on your father's cottage.'

'Why? Whatever did Lady Constance say?' Annie stared at him wondering what had possessed him.

'I have need of you here and I want you as far away from the hall as possible.'

He tucked a lock of her hair behind her ear and smiled at her.

'You can be of more help to me here, tending the mother and child. Lord Carrington and I have things that need to be sorted out.'

Annie was dumbfounded by his kindness.

'I will make sure your father is cared for,' he began again.

Annie rounded on him.

'Don't bother yourself. I can assure you he is making sure of that himself!'

Samuel looked at her, eyes wide at her sudden change of countenance.

'It is beyond words to say, but rest assured he has everything in hand.'

Annie was annoyed when she thought she had seen a fleeting smile cross Samuel's face as if he were humoured by her ill temper.

'There is more that I have not told you, Doctor Speer.'

Annie could barely find it in her heart to face him, but was sure any tendency to smile would be far removed once she told the whole truth. For sure, Lady Carrington had orchestrated an attempt to murder a member of his own flesh and blood.

'You may find it beyond your

capacity to believe, but I swear it is the truth. Georgette did not run away with the baby. She was sent, carried off into the night.'

'What is this?'

Lord Carrington's outrage shook both of them as he entered the room.

'Annie, tell us everything, please,' Samuel said, and placed a comforting hand on her shoulder.

Annie did but was not prepared for the rage that Lord Carrington flew into when she had finished.

'I will deal with this. Come, Samuel. Annie, see to my darling Georgette and her child.'

She nodded, but Samuel bent over and kissed her forehead.

'Do not fear, Annie, all will be well.'

'Will you go to the authorities?' Annie asked nervously, knowing full well that what had been said could not be withdrawn.

'Lord Carrington is the authority, Annie. He is a powerful man and one who has been most diabolically wronged.

It is now our job to set right that wrong.'

She watched the men depart and, looking at the baby, she prayed his words were true.

Outside, Carrington and Speer mounted their horses.

'Where to next?' Samuel asked.

Lord Carrington shouted over.

'To see Lady Constance. I have unfinished business. It is time she is informed of Lord Hallam's fall from grace.'

Annie opened the cottage door.

'Lady Constance left the hall. She headed south.'

'Then there is no time to waste. Where do you go, Samuel?'

'To find the boy, Jeremiah. I think I know who will tell me his whereabouts,' Samuel answered, nodding to Annie.

Both men departed at speed, leaving Annie to wait.

10

Lady Constance ordered the coach to make all haste to go to Kepstone Manor, the seat of her lover, Lord Carrington. Events had become intolerable. He was involved with Lord Hallam in their other business and he had power. What's more, Constance smiled knowingly, he was totally besotted with her and like an obedient pup within her hands. She would have him bark loud and clear to the dragoons, the magistrates and anyone who would care to listen that her trust and estate had been betrayed by the local rabble.

Why hadn't the bodies of Georgette, the child and Jeremiah been discovered, too? Edgar must know the full information on who had been found and where. She would have him tell her all there was to know and act quickly upon it. Lord Hallam would be returning to the estate the next day.

Constance nestled back into the padded seat of her carriage and pondered the enjoyment of the night before her. She was sure that he would have survived the planned accident. He had more lives than a cat. Amos was too crude in his attempts. He was adequate for removing troublesome peasants from the land, but not, it had been proved, sufficiently gifted of wit to remove more intelligent prey.

The coach slowed to a halt outside the Jacobean hall. The building did not appeal to her. It was too old and set in its style. She preferred to be at one with fashion and longed to live in the regal heart of London, attending court and wooing the pure-bred gentry. One day, she would be the toast of their fair city, and not be buried away in these cold, uncultured, sheep-rearing backwaters but alas, not yet.

Edwards was greeted by a manservant dressed in a fine uniform. They exchanged words and then Edwards returned to the carriage.

'Lord Carrington is not at home, Lady Hallam,' Edwards said in his normal sombre manner.

'When is he expected, Edwards?' Lady Constance asked as if she was having to waste her breath on asking the obvious question.

'He could not say, milady,' Edwards replied dryly.

'Then tell him to have a tray prepared for Lady Hallam and have it served to me in a comfortable and warmed room whilst I await his return. I am in shock and am in no fit state to return without refreshment!' Lady Constance snapped her order at Edwards.

'Yes, milady.'

He bowed and despatched her orders to the bemused man at the door. She watched Edwards exchange further words with the flustered servant and then he returned to the carriage yet again. He opened the door and lowered the steps.

'He will arrange for a place to be

found for you, milady, but thought it highly irregular. He was uncertain how his lordship would respond on his return.'

Constance sighed.

'That is of no concern of his. He is not paid to think on such issues but to obey.'

She strode boldly into the dark, wooded hallway, decorated with centuries-old weapons. It was not to her taste, but had the feel of a powerful man, an inheritance passed down the line from generation to generation. Yes, she thought, she could live in such a place if necessity dictated she should.

'This way, Lady Hallam.' The flustered man showed her into a room with many chairs, chaise longue and ornate furnishings. 'A tray will arrive shortly.'

She nodded then flicked her hand to dismiss him, as was her habit at the hall. She ruffled his pride, which delighted her.

'So who are you?'

The young, petulant voice took her

by surprise as a boy in sombre dress entered the room. He must have been not much beyond his tenth year, Constance thought.

'Why, who are you, young sir?'

Her friendly manner had the desired effect. His supercilious nose lifted slightly into the air.

She smiled sweetly at him.

'I am Lord Carrington's son and this is my manor,' he said boldly.

Lady Constance looked wide-eyed at him, not mocking his impertinent attitude, for here before her was a part of Edgar's life of which she knew nothing.

'Really, are you left here alone while your father is away?' she asked innocently.

'Of course. He is frequently out with one business or another.' He seated himself on a window seat and stared directly at her. 'How, ma'am, do you have his acquaintance?'

'He has business with my husband, Lord Hallam, sir, and I merely come on an errand of mercy. I think he may be able to help us with a slight problem we have encountered on our estates.'

'Perhaps I can help. You may call me Frederick.'

Constance positively beamed at the arrogant child who assumed too much, but who might provide the answer to some of the many questions that were filling her head.

'I wish you could, but I'm afraid it is to do with the blackguards of the night, the scourge of our area and every honest man.'

'Please continue, you have my undivided attention.'

Constance coughed slightly to hide a laugh that escaped her despite her best efforts. This child was beyond arrogance. He was vanity with no bounds. How she would love to crush his vile, opinionated spirit and stamp him under foot. Yet, in a strange way his nerve appealed to her.

'We have been robbed of a drab wagonette, the gamekeeper has been found dead and I have a servant missing, presumed lost on the moors. My estate has been violated and Lord Hallam is totally unaware of events until he returns the morrow. I sought the aid of your father in order to establish some semblance of law and order on my land. I fear there will be anarchy! You know what happened in France!'

'You poor soul. Do not fear. I shall have a room made up forthwith and you shall stay here until your husband returns. I shall have my man, Benjamin, ride over to the abbey road and make sure all trace of the rabble has been removed from the scene. If the dragoons are not already in action I shall send him to stir the blackguards up!'

Frederick was on his feet pointing a finger towards the ceiling to stress his indignation.

'You fill my heart with comfort, sir. But . . . '

'Please, you may call me Frederick

and I shall call you . . . '

'Lady Constance.'

She dipped her head slightly, thinking this imbecile could surely not be a blood relative of Edgar. His mother must have been of neurotic or unstable stock.

'You would need to send him to the moor road for that was where the wagon was found.'

'No, Lady Constance, you are misinformed, for I was one of those who found your man.'

Frederick held his hands behind his back, puffing out his chest as if it made him look a day older. He seemed pleased at the genuinely surprised look on Constance's face.

'I beg your pardon? You said you were one of those who found Amos?'

Lady Constance was on the brink of giving him the sharp edge of her tongue. If he was playing a game and living out some kind of fantasy she would put an abrupt end to his childish game.

'Yes, Lady Constance. I found Amos Kell after we had been delayed when a wheel had become loose on our carriage. Fortunately Benjamin is excellent at his job and saw the problem before we lost the wheel . . . no . . . nearly our lives.'

'Our lives?' Lady Constance raised a quizzical eyebrow.

'Yes. Father and I were delayed, as I explained, when first our journey was interrupted by some harlots begging their trade by the roadside. I was all for running them off the road, but Father has a failing in his nature. He has a softness of the heart which will undoubtedly be his undoing.'

Constance's mouth dropped slightly open as all was starting to fall into place in her mind.

'These women. It is an odd place for women of the night to ply their trade, I should imagine.'

She looked at the youth who hesitated for a moment whilst he re-evaluated their description.

'Well, perhaps I should have said that that is what the one with child certainly was, for I am sure she had not a husband. They could have been runaways from the asylum for all I know. Anyway, Father decided to help them. Then one collapsed on the floor of our best carriage.' Frederick curled up his lips at the memory of it. 'Even the blanket was wrapped around the child and this on a freezing night.'

He shrugged at the irrationality of it all.

'Are they still here?' Constance asked innocently.

'My goodness, no! I would never allow such a thing. My ancestors would turn in their graves. No, they were dropped off at the village surgeon's cottage.'

Lady Constance swallowed. She realised that she was in grave danger.

'This surgeon, his name, would it be Speer?'

'Yes, that was it. We left the rabble there and Father reported the wagon and your man. Now, would you care to take tea with me?'

He smiled, well pleased with himself.

'Alas, I cannot possibly. I realise that my presence here is an imposition.'

She turned her head towards the door.

'Edwards!' she called, knowing the man would be outside the door awaiting her command. He duly appeared.

'Yes, milady?'

'Fetch the carriage, we will be leaving forthwith.' Lady Constance was swiftly out of the door.

'What do I tell Father?' Frederick asked, not understanding.

'Nothing, for sure, young sir. He will rebuke you for saying too much already.'

Lady Constance climbed into the carriage. As soon as they were out of earshot of the hall and servants she gave her order to Edwards.

'York, and make haste!'

11

Samuel headed straight for Thomas Fletcher's cottage. If Thomas didn't know where the boy was then he would have a good idea. Also, Muriel was no innocent young woman like Annie. She was the type who would have an ear for all the gossip. If Annie's safety was under threat, then he was sure he could get them to talk to him. He was not far from his own cottage when he was amazed to see the breathless figure of Thomas trudging toward him.

'Whatever are you doing here, Thomas?'

Samuel dismounted and stood before the man as he breathed heavily.

'I have to speak with her. She should never have seen me like that with Muriel. Annie deserves better, but I felt so well and, and . . . I . . . '

Thomas looked around him, anywhere but at Samuel.

'Whatever has distressed you so? Annie is safe at my cottage at the moment but there is a matter I must speak to you about most urgently.'

Samuel was amazed when Thomas put both hands over his face and sobbed.

'I am a man in torment. I am sorry, Samuel. What must you think of me?'

'Whatever have you done, Samuel? Can it be this bad?'

'Annie hasn't told you, has she?'

Samuel shook his head.

'She walked in when I and Muriel were . . . we were . . . She has made me feel so much better and I do love her.'

Samuel put his hand on Thomas's shoulder.

'You must speak with your daughter urgently and try to put things right between you. She has been through enough recently.'

'I know, Doctor, I know.' Thomas nodded.

'You do not know the half of it, Thomas. I would ask you, talk quietly. I have a sick woman and a baby in my home. I wish no more distress to be brought to them than they have already endured.'

'No, of course not. If she will let me in I'll be brief. I am to marry Muriel. Her brother, Arthur, knows but I have found it difficult to tell Annie. She loved her mother so.'

Samuel mounted his horse once more.

'I understand, Thomas, I really do. However, if you want to save Annie even more distress, there is information that you must give me.'

'Anything.'

Thomas wiped his eyes and looked up at Samuel.

'I need to know where I can find the boy, Jeremiah.'

Samuel saw Thomas look down instantly.

'I don't know where the boy is.'

'Thomas, if you don't, would the man Jeb Webb?'

Thomas's answer was swift.

'You don't want to cross his path, Samuel. He's a man with a temper and little charity.'

'It will help Annie to clear herself from a mess not of her making, but sadly involving her and the woman in my care.'

'Go to the last cottage in Beckton. Knock twice, then once, wait to the count of ten and knock one more time. Muriel will answer the door. She'll take you to him because you have been entrusted with one of Beckton's many secrets.'

Thomas was staring at the ground at his feet.

'Thank you, friend,' Samuel replied.

'Don't thank me, man. No-one would send a friend to Jeb uninvited. Pray God you return safely.'

Samuel left with much on his mind but determined to see the matter through to conclusion.

* * *

When Annie heard the knock on the door, she thought it must be Lord Carrington, and answered it with great relief — until she saw her father's face. She was about to slam the door shut but he was quick, anticipating her reaction. He held it ajar, then edged his way in.

'We have to talk, Annie.'

She shut the door, closed the shutters on Georgette's room and then pointed toward the kitchen. He entered and sat down at the table. She felt he was tired. He looked it and despite her anger and disgust with him, she poured him a drink.

'I have nothing to stay to you.'

She sat down and stared in the opposite direction to him, making sure she was out of arm's reach. She didn't want to feel his touch.

'I can understand the way you feel,' he began.

'I don't think for one instant you could, Father,' she said and folded her arms defiantly.

'I do! I love her. I want to marry her,

but you're always so dismissive of her. She's cared for me whilst you were at the hall . . .'

'Yes, I can see that, but I was there to keep the Hallam's from sending you to the debtors' gaol!'

Annie raised her voice in anger then remembered about Georgette and Bethany.

'I am fully aware of that and you will have my undying gratitude, but loving Muriel does not mean that I did not or have stopped loving your mother. They are totally different, but I want to be loved again.'

Annie opened her mouth to speak, but her father raised his hand to stop her.

'I am a man, Annie. I need the love of a good woman, and Muriel is a good woman. You just never give her a chance to show it to you.'

He looked down. Annie felt a tear escape and roll down her cheek but she could not force one word out of her mouth. She had too many confused and strange emotions running around inside her head.

‘I’m sorry, Annie. I’ve let you down and for that I am heartily sorry. I ask you to forgive me for not handling events better. I hope when you meet a man whom you really deeply love and desire, you will understand and forgive me. I want to live a life of happiness again in my humble home. It is yours, too, and will always be so.’

She let him leave without a word spoken between them. She cried. His words had hurt, more than he could have known. She felt betrayed. She realised she had known he liked Muriel and that was why she had not encouraged the woman. That was unfair. But she did know what it was like to love, and want and because of social ranking to be excluded from him.

She wanted Samuel Speer. She longed for him to wrap his arms around her and to be done with this mess. But she could not have whom she wanted so would remain a maid, as no farmhand had ever made her feel alive, like one glance or touch from the good doctor had.

'Oh, yes, Father. I understand,' she muttered miserably to herself.

'There's no-one here, Annie.'

The familiar, delicate voice made her jump out of the chair.

'Georgette!'

Annie flung her arms around her friend with joy, and baby Bethany started to cry.

* * *

Lady Constance was in a blind fury. They had been so near to making a fortune, one that would have taken them into London Society. Every ambition she had wanted to fulfil over the last few intolerable years of marriage had been within her grasp and was now threatened.

The buffoon of a husband of hers had needed her to orchestrate the most lucrative of his businesses and he had risked it all because of his irrational desire for an heir. Why, when he had her?

It would have served him right if the

wench had provided him with a useless milksop like Frederick Carrington. She would have laughed at the thought of such a futile specimen being under her maternal supervision if it had not been for the gravity of the information he had so readily imparted to her. Everything she had planned had come to a staggering and blinding halt. No sooner had the thought crossed her mind than the coach pulled to a stop. She was almost thrown unceremoniously on to the floor.

'What's the meaning of this?'

Edwards's voice was heard loud and clear. However, silence followed. Lady Constance peeked out of the window to see a group of ruffians on horseback ahead of the coach, pistols pointed at Edwards. She removed the small pistol from her pelisse only to have the opposite door of the carriage flung open and the pistol ripped from her hand.

'Edgar! What is the meaning of this outrage?'

Constance's indignation was as false

as her heart but she was a born survivor and, despite what this man may now know of her, she had bedded him. He was besotted with her. She had pleased him and she believed he truly was under her sensuous spell.

'They are a few acquaintances of ours, Constance.'

He moved into the carriage, sitting down opposite her. He banged the roof and the carriage continued to proceed on its way.

'I am delighted to see you, Edgar, even though your entry is somewhat dramatic. I have just departed from Kepstone Hall. I . . . '

'I know. It is a shame you had not awaited my arrival. I'm sure Frederick would have kept you entertained until then.'

Constance rubbed her knee against his, looking at him impishly from under her lids.

'Don't flatter yourself, woman!'

His reply cut her like a knife. No-one had ever dared refer to her in such a manner, nor refuse her advances in such a heavy-handed way.

'Have you forgotten whom you address, Edgar?'

'I have neither forgotten whom or what I am addressing, nor shall I ever forget again, not even for crown and country.'

'Are you really trying to tell me that you did not fall in love with me as you sold your little secrets on, Edgar?'

She was feeling uneasy, muscles tensing within her. An unusual feeling of insecurity was making her tremble slightly. If he was an agent of the Crown, her life was in the balance. She had sought to warn Lord Hallam so they could make their escape with his money in London, but now her intentions were sighted on her saving her own neck.

'I am not trying to tell you, woman. I am informing you that as an agent of the Crown you are now under arrest.'

He showed nothing but disdain for her.

In a desperate attempt to affect his heart once more she flung herself on his lap.

'No, Edgar, it was my husband who made me do everything. He is an ambitious man. You know how much older than I he is, and he made me do everything.'

Her sobbing was pitiful, but genuine, as she had no wish to be thrown in prison, or worse, die.

'And Georgette, did he make you send her and her newborn out into the depth of the night with an assassin for a chaperone?'

'Yes, yes, yes!' she lied, with such mock sincerity that she almost convinced herself it was true.

The coach stopped and he pushed her away from him with a sharp thrust. Her hair, usually immaculate, lost a pin and became a dishevelled mess.

'Where are we?' Panic welled up inside her.

'York, where you wanted to go, wasn't it?' He half-smiled.

'Yes, Edgar, it is. I'll take you to Lord Hallam. He's at his club. He'll tell you I was an innocent pawn in this, no more.'

'Less, I'm afraid.'

He flung open the door to reveal four dragoons standing with arms ready to escort her.

'Your husband is already in his new abode awaiting your arrival, although I doubt you will share a joint suite, Constance.'

'You monster! I'll tell them everything you did, and more.'

She spat at his face as she stepped out. It was with total shock that he tripped her foot causing her to fall flat on the muddied cobbles. He didn't even look to see her pulled to her feet and marched inside. She tried one last desperate attempt to touch his heart.

'Edgar, don't abandon me!'

The coach moved away, and all was lost.

12

Samuel knocked on the door of the cottage in the manner that Thomas had carefully described. It opened, and Muriel's mouth dropped open in shock when she saw Samuel's face.

'What be you doin' that for?'

She peered behind him, looking around to see if anyone else had seen his arrival.

'I think you know, Muriel. I wish to meet someone of your acquaintance.'

'Stop yer blabbin', man, and come in. Do you think I want everyone knowin' me business?'

He entered the small cottage and was promptly seated at a table. She scratched her head under her bonnet.

'Look, you best be out of 'ere. You are a good man and I'll not see yer harmed in any way, but you must go now.'

'I need to speak with the boy, Jeremiah, the boy from Hallam Hall. He's hiding somewhere and he has no need to. Can you help me to find him?'

She clasped her hands together, shaking her head.

'Oh, lad, you are chasin' a lost cause. He was shot, accidentally like, when he ran through the woods after he crashed the wagon. They tried to save him, honest, but it was no good. He's gone, and in a manner of speakin' you should go, too. You don't want to be mixed up with Jeb, no way. He's not your type of man at all.'

'That saddens me. I don't hold with slavery and I'd hoped to offer the boy a decent life. I would have had him help me.'

He sighed but looked around the small cottage. Something made him uneasy.

'Muriel, if you're the right woman for Thomas, and I understand you are, then surely he is not the kind of person you would wish to be entangled with local villains either.'

He watched her grin broadly and, although he was sorry he had not been able to help the boy, he felt for Annie's sake he wanted to help Thomas and Muriel extricate themselves from this wicked man's grip on the village.

'You do talk nice, sir. We cannot get ourselves out of this. We know too much, you see. We stay silent or we are silenced. That's the way of it.'

'Who is this elusive Jeb? For him to disappear like he does, he must masquerade as this person, but be someone known in the village by day. Why can no-one describe him?'

Samuel could not believe such a small community had lived under the threat of one man for such a time. Then the obvious thought struck.

'Is he real, Muriel? Does he exist or is he more than one man? You always have food to share with Thomas, and he's never gone without. If he paid his rent, it would be extremely obvious that the village was funding itself in other ways other than from the estate. You're all part of it, aren't you?'

Muriel turned away.

'Would you have a drink, lad?'

'Don't change the subject. Am I right, or not?'

'You are, but you have to let the matter drop, Samuel, or there will be trouble.'

Thomas's voice out of the blue surprised him, but in a way it made sense. He was a clever man. He must have figured it out long since. Perhaps that was why Dr Brown dulled his senses. He was in the pay of the gang.

'You made a speedy return, Thomas.' Samuel stared at him.

'I used the old monks' tracks. They're overgrown mostly, but locals know many a path through the woods unseen to a stranger.'

'It has to stop — the trade. You're known for smuggling expertise, but haven't killed, yet, except for Jeremiah.'

Thomas looked at Muriel.

'Let him have the child. He will not hurt him.'

Muriel shrugged her shoulders and opened a small cupboard to reveal a hiding hole behind it. The youth uncurled his limbs and blinked as he came out into the dusky light of the cottage. Samuel saw a blood stain on his shirt. He saw the wound had been bound, but needed proper tending.

'I didn't lie much. The lad was shot — well, grazed,' Muriel excused herself.

Samuel looked at the youth.

'You will stay in my household now.'

Jeremiah nodded as Samuel continued.

'Thomas, the dragoons are closing in on this area. The coastguards are to be brought in on every headland. Tell your contacts to cease their activities now or there will be blood spilled and ultimately it will be theirs.'

'Why do you do this for us? Why warn us?' Thomas asked.

'I do not want you implicated when trouble comes and, believe me, it is coming. Both Lord and Lady Hallam will be under arrest. Once they start talking and add their side of events to what Dr Brown has already said, the area will be combed. Send word, clean yourselves from the vile trade and say nothing of this conversation.' Samuel stood up. 'I must go now. Did you make amends with your daughter, Thomas?'

'I hope so. Time will tell.'

He put a protective arm around Muriel and squeezed her to him. Samuel smiled.

'Good day.'

'She's a good woman,' Thomas said.

'I've already said as much to her,' Samuel answered and looked to Muriel.

'I know that,' Thomas said, 'but I meant my Annie.'

Samuel nodded and opened the door.

'I know what you meant, Thomas.'

* * *

Annie watched Bethany being held properly by her mother for the first time and it overwhelmed her with joy, despite her own private turmoil. The child suckled from its mother's breast and to Annie it was the most marvellous thing she had ever seen. Georgette, free of her torment, relaxed, could only thank Annie repeatedly for seeing her through everything.

'I could do nothing, Georgette. I followed Lady Hallam's instructions like a puppet. All those months I betrayed you knowing that she planned to keep a boy child. I didn't know what to do.'

'You did everything and more than you could have done. When you ran out into the night, you risked your own life, Annie. We are forever indebted to you. Now, you have brought us to Samuel. We have such plans. He is qualified now. We shall go to Whitby.'

Georgette's eyes shone so bright, her smile so broad, that Annie could only admire the woman's beauty, thus far subdued.

'I am delighted for you both.'

Annie forced herself to share her

friend's enthusiasm, even though her own heart felt devoid of any love or purpose. She heard Samuel open the cottage door. As he greeted his cousin with delight and relief, she took Jeremiah to the kitchen and cleaned his arm. It was cut, but not badly.

'It's good to see you, Jeremiah.'

Annie saw the pleasure in his eyes as she spoke to him.

'You, too, miss. Is the baby fine?'

He looked toward the door, a concerned expression across his face.

'She is fine, like her mother. They need to build strength, but now their ordeal is over.'

'I'm to go to Whitby with Dr Speer. I'm to assist him. He says he can use my brains as well as my muscle but he intends to pay me, miss.'

'That's wonderful, Jeremiah.'

Annie finished her chore and gave him some bread and cheese. Then she poured him an ale.

'Enjoy this. I have to go and see my father, Jeremiah. Will you thank Dr

Samuel for all that he has done? I don't want to disturb them. They have much to talk about.'

Annie wrapped her shawl around her shoulders and left quietly. It was some minutes before Samuel realised she was no longer in the cottage, when Lord Carrington entered and greeted Georgette with a warm embrace.

'Edgar! My nightmare has gone, but I am disgraced. I . . . '

Georgette's voice broke and she hugged her baby to her.

'No, Georgette, we both fell foul of an evil woman. It should never happen again. My work here is done. As soon as you are strong enough, we shall wed discreetly, and you shall be announced at my new residence in Whitby as my wife and Bethany my child. All will be well now, my love. I give you my sworn word. No-one shall treat you or Bethany so ill again.'

* * *

Annie walked aimlessly along the familiar road towards the hall. She would collect her few possessions and speak with Cook, then make her way to another village or town. It mattered not. Wherever she went now, she would have to start her life over from nothing.

She heard horse's hooves approaching from behind and stepped off the road to let it pass. It didn't.

'Where are your manners, woman? Would you leave my house without a fitting goodbye?'

Dr Speer dismounted and waited for her to return to the road.

'I left a message with Jeremiah,' Annie answered, in no mood for rebukes or arguments.

'So I heard, but why?'

'You were busy. I did not want to get in the way. You all have so many plans to make. You have Georgette and I'm very happy for you, and the baby. Jeremiah is thrilled you are giving him a fresh start. I have no place being there so . . . '

'Decided all by yourself to go.' He placed a hand behind her head. 'Look at me, Annie Fletcher.'

She stared at his dark features, his eyes, and almost wanted to kiss his moist lips. As the thought crossed her mind, she pulled away.

'I want you to be with me,' he said. 'I have a dream to help the impoverished by using my skills and charging those who can pay well for my services. I need someone who is strong, someone who has integrity, whom I can trust, to work at my side.' He paused.

'Georgette is all and everything that you have described,' Annie answered quietly.

'I couldn't agree more, but she will marry Edgar. They will have many little children, no doubt, and be sickeningly happy, and I am delighted in this.'

He spun her around and held her shoulders. The horse's reins slipped from his hand.

'But I, too, need a good woman, and you are that unique person, Annie.'

'You hardly know me. I am from poor stock and dubious parentage and you are an educated man of means, Samuel. You have no need of Annie Fletcher!'

She stared at him, her anguish replaced by annoyance as he smiled back at her. Was he mocking her? He continued.

'It took all the money we had left to us to pay for my education which was why Georgette took a position in the first place. She had previously looked after Frederick.' Samuel sighed. 'This was an awful mistake. Edgar fell in love with her, but Frederick was so repugnant she was sent away. It was thought to be a safe position at Hallam Hall for her. We had one letter of her distress at events there, then nothing. Georgette vanished. Lord Carrington was told by Lady Constance that she packed her bags and left without notice.'

He pulled her to him, enveloping her in his arms.

'Other worldly events had moved forward at such a pace that Edgar realised he had a major case to follow through at Hallam.'

'So you came here.'

'As soon as I could. Annie, will you come with me? Your actions have told me all I need to know about your character. I care not about your breeding or status. You are educated and . . . ' He kissed her lips.

Annie responded to her own feelings and inner desires.

'And, Doctor Speer?'

'Annie, please. Marry me? Share my life, my dream. You shall never regret it.'

'This is very sudden, Samuel. Are you sure?'

'Annie Fletcher, I am a decisive man. Would you have me ask your father?'

'Absolutely not!' Annie was appalled at the suggestion.

'Then think for yourself. What do you want? What does your heart and head tell you? Are they at one with each other?'

'Yes, Samuel, I will,' Annie answered joyfully, flinging her arms around his neck.

He lifted her up to place her in the saddle, then swung up behind her.

'Should we tell your father now?' he asked as he kicked the horse on down the road.

'Not yet. That will take a little more time to put right,' Annie answered as she hung on tightly to him.

From now on, Annie was going to live her life for herself and not for anyone else, except for Samuel, Georgette, Bethany and Jeremiah. She laughed out loud.

'What is so funny or are you just happy?' Samuel asked.

'Go by my father's cottage. We shall indeed tell him, wish him and Muriel well then we can break the news to Georgette.'

Samuel nodded.

'I knew I'd chosen a wise woman. I

love you, Annie Fletcher, and I'll make you happy, I swear.'

'You already have.'

Annie hugged him tightly, truly happy for the first time in her life.

THE END

Other titles in the
Linford Romance Library:

FAITHFUL TO A DREAM

Sheila Holroyd

Beth was fiercely loyal to Charles Stuart as he fought to regain his dead father's throne, even though it brought her into conflict with Tom Everard, the man she was growing to love. Her desire to help the would-be king brought her danger and disillusionment. Reality did not match her dreams, but Tom was there to help her and to teach her how to find happiness in a country divided by civil war.

LOVE'S LOST TREASURE

Joyce Johnson

When Rosie Treloar discovers her fiancé is an unscrupulous conman, she flees London for her native Cornwall. Here, she takes a job as a tourist guide and meets American Ben Goodman, who is researching the mystery of his family's legacy, lost during the English Civil War. Rosie, increasingly attracted to Ben, becomes involved with his mission, unaware that there are other sinister forces seeking the legacy — forces which could threaten her newfound happiness with Ben . . .